She twisted around to take a look at the person who was going to accompany her on this assignment.

The pressure in the room changed, condensed. The man was six feet of raw energy in a tightly muscled package...clipped to his belt was the gold NCIS badge. The telltale bulge on the other side of him indicated that he was carrying a sidearm. His thick black hair covered his forehead, errant tendrils curling along the nape of his neck.

Sia gasped as she looked into steady, beautiful dark gray eyes, eyes that had gazed into hers full of a smoky passion that only made them darken.

Oh, damn.

Chris Vargas.

Her brother's wingman.

The very pilot who had been directly responsible for her brother's death.

Dear Reader,

Sexy NCIS agents, tough JAG lawyers, rogue navy SEALs, courageous marines—a mix of navy and civilians investigating murder, espionage and crime across a global landscape. These are the characters that will be the fodder for my new series for Romantic Suspense, To Protect and Serve!

At His Command throws together former lovers Chris and Sia. He was her brother's wingman and a cocky up-and-coming navy pilot until he made a mistake and crashed into his wingman's fighter jet, killing him. Now, six years later, as a JAG lawyer, Sia is ordered to work with an NCIS agent who turns out to be Chris. They must investigate the death of a high-profile pilot on Chris's former post—the aircraft carrier *U.S.S. James McCloud*. He must face not only the memories of that fateful day, but the woman who was as affected by the tragedy as he—one she hasn't recovered from. As they try to track down a killer in uniform, will they be able to overcome their painful past and find a future together?

I look forward to creating more great characters in my upcoming novels for the To Protect and Serve miniseries. In the meantime, buckle up and hold on while I kick in the afterburners for a wild ride in *At His Command*.

Best,

Karen

KAREN ANDERS

At His Command

ROMANTIC
SUSPENSE

Recycling programs
for this product may
not exist in your area.

ISBN-13: 978-0-373-27783-4

AT HIS COMMAND

www.Harlequin.com

Printed in U.S.A.

Books by Karen Anders

Harlequin Romantic Suspense

Five-Alarm Encounter #1658
*At His Command #1713

*To Protect and Serve

KAREN ANDERS

is a three-time National Readers' Choice Award final-ist and *RT Book Reviews* Reviewers' Choice finalist, and has won a prestigious Holt Medallion. Two of her novels made the Waldenbooks bestseller list in 2003. Published since 1997, she currently writes romantic suspense for Harlequin Books. To contact the author, please write to her in care of Harlequin Books, 233 Broadway, Suite 1001, New York, NY 10279, or visit www.karenanders.com.

To Kero, for real friendship and for helping me
kill virtual monsters.

Chapter 1

"Aren't you Rafael Soto's sister?"

Sia bristled. She *had* been his sister, but now she was Lieutenant Commander Ambrosia Soto, U.S. Navy JAG. Most of her friends called her Sia, but she didn't think Master Chief Steven Walker was acting at all friendly toward her right now.

He was her number-one suspect in the death of a decorated F/A-18 pilot whose body had been recovered from the bottom of the Pacific, and the man had gone from helpful to belligerent as soon as he discovered who she was. A Navy JAG lawyer often had that effect on guilty people.

The tone of the man's voice said he wasn't a fan of her brother, but highly trained and aggressive fighter pilots were often considered elite jerks by the enlisted.

Ending up on an aircraft carrier in the Pacific was a common occurrence for a JAG officer. She'd been to many places around the globe, handling all types of legal issues and investigations. She took this assignment in stride. She had been on temporary assignment duty, or TAD, investigating another case in San Diego when she'd been ordered to handle this investigation aboard the aircraft carrier *U.S.S. James McCloud*— her brother's last billet. "You can address me as Commander Soto or ma'am."

"But you're his sister, right?"

"Master Chief, are you not getting my drift? I'm here to ask the questions, not answer them." She flipped open his file and glanced down. The picture and material were all neatly maintained. She looked up at him and narrowed her eyes. "This investigation is about Lieutenant Malcolm Saunders, who lost his life yesterday when his F/A-18 Super Hornet plunged into the sea. It's not social hour."

Her sharp words seemed to glance off him. "Yeah, you'd know about fighter jet accidents, wouldn't you?"

She shot him a cold look and a smoldering fury burned beneath her skin. She maintained eye contact with his direct ones with a relentless stare, as if doing so would give her an insight into his soul. She was rewarded as he looked away, but before he did, she saw a challenge and the unmistakable look of a liar. Her scalp prickled and the hair on the back of her neck stood up. She always got that feeling when someone was hiding something. Almost like a sixth sense.

She picked up his folder and studied the man's service record, looking for any inconsistencies. "We both know you didn't get to your rank by being uncooperative, Master Chief." At her statement, he sat up straighter. "In fact, you have a spotless service record. The Navy is your life and you've given to it unconditionally."

For a moment, deep regret filled his eyes, but when he blinked they were once again neutral. "I have, sometimes to the detriment of all else."

"And the Navy has given back. You head up Maintenance Material Control."

"Yes."

"Maintenance is the heart of this carrier. Your division is responsible for repairing aircraft and related support equipment."

"Yes."

"One of the branches you oversee is the avionics division?"

"I do."

"Were there any problems with any part of the systems your people maintain?" She set the file down and closed it.

For a moment, the master chief sat in silence, but she could see something she said had caused him concern. But his next words were contrary to the worry he tried to hide. "No. That plane was in tip-top condition."

She lifted her brows and tilted her head. "Yet the pilot and the plane ended up at the bottom of the ocean. How do you explain that?"

"Pilot error."

Sia couldn't help it. She winced and the look on the master chief's face made Sia want to make him pay for his scored hit. "I've been assigned to investigate the reason a forty-million-dollar jet crashed into the ocean and killed the pilot. Lieutenant Saunders was in charge of flying the plane. You were in charge of maintaining the plane. Therefore, I'm asking you questions. I suggest you answer." The authority in her voice was unmistakable. The master chief's lips tightened at her tone.

"I know I'm responsible for the maintenance of the plane. But you have the logs—"

"And I'll inspect them thoroughly. Thank you, Master Chief."

He got to the door, opened it and stopped, his body language aggressive. His aftershave mixed with the unmistakable scent of the ocean and the metallic smell of the ship. A slight breeze ruffled the hair at her nape that had escaped her tight bun.

"Why aren't you looking at pilot error? Are you so sure the pilot didn't make a mistake?"

"I run a thorough investigation. I'll get to the truth of the accident." She rose and set her hands on the small table she'd been sitting behind. "My way."

"Maybe you have a mental block regarding pilot error, Commander Soto?" he said with a soft, accusing tone.

Something snapped in Sia. She was across the small compartment and in the master chief's face before she could stop herself.

"It's no secret what happened with my brother, and it's no secret regarding my insistence for a reopening of the investigation into the incident. I will not have you impugning my integrity. If you do so again, I'll bring you up on charges. Is that clear?"

"Yes, ma'am," he said, his anger barely banked.

"You are dismissed."

Sia had been in the JAG Corps long enough to understand respect was due an officer and some of the good ol' boys left over from the old system didn't take very well to a woman in command. But with the master chief, Sia was sure he had more to hide than his distaste for women in uniform. She had only to prove it.

Maybe you have a mental block...

The master chief's words made her angry all over again. Sia trusted in her brother's abilities as a pilot. When the JAG who'd investigated her brother's F/A-18 accident cited pilot error, Sia had protested loudly. But it did no good. Now six years later, Sia was in another battle. She'd petitioned to have her brother's ashes memorialized at the Naval War Memorial and was promptly told by the official she talked to it wasn't possible. Her brother hadn't died a hero.

That meant she'd have to get her brother's case reopened and that took an appeal to the Secretary of the Navy, or as he was referred to at JAG, SECNAV.

She didn't blame the War Memorial. She blamed the wingman who'd flown with her brother—the man with whom she'd had the most explosive, intimate relationship in her life. Even six years later, the thought of him made her heart beat faster and her palms sweat. She didn't want this reaction, but she couldn't seem to stop it. That promising relationship had ended with her brother's fatal accident.

The loss of her brother had torn her family apart, and she'd simply lost everything except work. The JAG Corps and her job sustained her and honed her into a legal killing machine. Focusing her thoughts back to the investigation, she asked the ship's resident JAG to send in the next person for questioning. In this case, it was the pilot's wingman.

The master chief hesitated when he saw Lieutenant Saunders's wingman standing silently but attentively through their exchange at the door. Then he said something softly under his breath and strode off down the corridor, ducking through the hatch.

Sia focused on the man in front of her in his crisp khaki uniform and aviator's flight jacket. "Lieutenant Russell, thank you for your time."

"I hope it helped in the investigation." His voice was subdued, the grief at the loss of his friend and wingman poignant. Unexpectedly, Sia's throat filled as a result of the memories of the day she'd lost her brother all in one terrible fiery crash. It was the same day she had lost the man she loved, her brother's wingman, who had ejected to safety. "Mal and I were more than wing mates. We were best friends."

"I am very sorry for your loss."

"Thank you, ma'am."

He stepped into the compartment and she shut the door. She indicated the chair in front of the table. "Have a seat." When he was settled and she'd taken her own seat again, she said, "Can you tell me about Lieutenant Saunders's state of mind yesterday when his jet crashed into the ocean?"

He smiled, his eyes brightening. "He was psyched. We always were when we got to fly."

Sia leaned back in her chair. "Anything happen that was out of the ordinary?"

Lieutenant Russell frowned. "The only thing that happened wasn't out of the ordinary."

"What is that?"

He sighed. "Master Chief Walker always seemed to be in Mal's face."

"They didn't get along?"

"No. The master chief was always using what we liked to call good-natured ribbing to put him down, and Mal just ignored his behavior."

"Do you know why the master chief had this perspective?" Sia asked.

"No, ma'am. It seemed to manifest from the first day Mal and I were assigned to this ship."

Sia looked down at the open folder. "I don't see any reprimands in the master chief's file."

Lieutenant Russell shrugged. "Mal wasn't like that. He held his own, he told me. He didn't need to tattle to the Navy command because an enlisted sailor didn't like him. He was as perplexed as I was as to why the master chief immediately singled him out for abuse. We revere master chiefs in the Navy. They know just about every damn thing there is to know. We just didn't get it."

"He should have reported him."

Lieutenant Russell's shoulders drooped and his voice grew strained. "I agree, ma'am. But, Mal is...I mean was Mal."

"Is there any other information you can provide that might help the investigation?" She saw him hesitate and look down as he ran his fingers along the brim of his hat, debating. "Anything," she prompted. "No matter how small and insignificant."

He looked up. The anguish on his face twisted Sia's heart. Her memories were still painful, as if her brother had died yesterday instead of six years ago. Fresh pain flooded through her. "Lieutenant Russell?"

"I hope I'm not talking out of turn, ma'am, but I saw the master chief near Mal's coffee before we took off."

"In the wardroom? Enlisted personnel aren't allowed in there," Sia said.

"No, Mal was just about to step onto the flight deck, and he was finishing it off." He set his hat on the table and leaned forward, his voice dropping. "I don't want to accuse him of tampering with it, but Mal was a top-notch aviator and there's no way in hell he would have downed that plane like that."

"Are you willing to sign an oath to that, Lieutenant?"

"Yes, ma'am. I will." He held her gaze and never wavered, clearly a man who was dedicated to both his friend and the Navy.

Sia dismissed Lieutenant Russell and she moved quickly. She contacted the captain via the ship's phone and requested a search authorization for the master chief's rack, citing the evidence from Lieutenant Russell's oath. With his permission, Sia made her way to the master chief's quarters with a burly master-at-arms in tow. Once inside, she started to methodically search his locker. She found nothing. Sure that she had missed something, she started the search once again. As she went through his underwear and socks, she was about to give up. Her hand brushed against a sock and she felt a hard lump. Fishing out the sock, Sia pulled the garments apart and a bottle fell out onto the deck. Reaching down, she picked it up. When she turned the label toward her, she found she held an over-the-counter product for irregularity.

Her brows furrowed as she looked down at the bright yellow bottle. Why was this in his sock drawer and not in the medicine cabinet? Then it dawned on her. He was trying to hide it.

She would have the contents of the bottle analyzed against anything that was in Lieutenant Saunders's bloodstream. She could be holding the murder weapon in her hand. The hairs on the back of her neck prickled and goose bumps ran along her back and arms.

She needed to detain the master chief and talk to the ME who was doing the autopsy right away.

She motioned for the master-at-arms to follow her as she headed to the legal office to log the evidence and contact the ME. She dismissed the master-at-arms once she reached the office.

When there was a knock at the door, Sia rose to open it. The sea rolled and as the carrier dipped, she lost her balance and got turned around. The door slipped out of her hands. When it popped open, someone shoved her from behind hard enough to send her face-first against the far bulkhead of the office. Her head struck metal with a clanging sound that reverberated against her skull, rattling her brain. Stars exploded behind her eyes. Before she could recover from the suddenness of the push, her assailant hit her with a stunning blow to the back of the head and Sia fell into darkness.

When she woke up, she could taste blood in her mouth and smell the sea air. She opened one eye; the other one, swollen and throbbing, took a bit longer. She focused on a man sitting cross-legged in front of her. Unlike her he was dressed for the weather and the rough seas. Along with his outerwear, he had taken precautions and donned a bright orange life vest. Her hands were tied with a piece of rope in a knot that any sailor would know and that was impossible to untie. Fear sliced through her like the icy wind that battered her hair and exposed skin. She'd never been this open to the elements on the carrier, and it seemed as if they could touch the dark, clouded night sky.

"Master Chief."

"I'm afraid you've stuck your nose where it doesn't belong and your actions have caused me to remember my duty. I'm sorry about this, but you'll have to die."

"Your duty?" Sia spit out. "Murdering an officer is your duty?"

"I can't let you reopen old wounds. Your brother's 'accident' was pilot error just like Saunders's 'accident.'" He raised his hand and shook the bottle.

Sia shifted and studied the determined man before her. He wasn't telling her everything. She got that prickly feeling, only this time more urgently. She wasn't sure if it was because she was in a terrible position.

"Are you saying you had something to do with my brother's death?"

He set the bottle down with secrets in his eyes. "Nope. Not saying it. What I have to say doesn't matter where you're going." He rose and jerked her up by her arm with a painful grip. He pushed her to the edge of the sponson, a platform hanging on the side of the carrier, just below the flight deck. It was a sheer drop to the ocean. The plunge would kill her instantly.

"How did you get me up here with no one seeing?" she asked breathlessly as the ocean churned below her.

He laughed. "I know this ship like no one else. I have my ways. Enough talking. Say hi to Rafael for me."

Sia didn't give the man a chance to push her over. She lashed back with her booted foot and caught Walker right in the kneecap. She heard the bottle roll away against the bulkhead. Walker howled, but the wind whipped the words away. No amount of yelling would bring anyone up here.

He tried to backhand her, but Sia was ready, balancing on the balls of her feet. She ducked, came up with her bound hands and jabbed him in the sternum. He swung widely, sending him off balance. Sia dodged out of the way and Walker's momentum took him over the rail, his scream of rage and fear drowned out by the wind and the ocean.

The soft breeze off the ocean touched her face as she heard the screen door open and close. Remnants of her celebratory graduation party fluttered in the breeze on the table situated on the patio.

As she glanced over, she expected to see her father, but instead a tall, dark-haired man carved out a piece of her cake and sat down.

Sia studied the strong line of his jaw, the width of his broad shoulders encased in Navy khaki. Drawn to him, she sauntered over and he looked up, capturing her with gray eyes as elusive and intriguing as smoke. She said nothing as she straddled his lap, the sun warm on her shoulders, the texture of his uniform stimulating on her fingertips. He smiled, the hint of frosting on his lips tantalizing. Her head dipped down and covered his mouth, the sweet taste of the frosting and him sending her mind into a free fall.

Warmth filtered through her, his groan soft and uncontrollable as he pressed his body against her. His mouth was hot, the press of flesh erotic and needy. If only she could get closer, hang on to the sensation, maybe she could forget what he had done. Forget...

"Miss?"

Sia tried to swim up from the dream, the memory of his mouth on hers.

"Miss? Are you all right?"

The flight attendant's worried face peered down at Sia.

"I'm fine," Sia said, but then she moved and the sore muscles of her arms, face and right shoulder reminded her she wasn't.

"Would you like some water? You were whimpering in your sleep."

Sia closed her eyes to hide her embarrassment. She looked around. Right, she was on the flight back to Norfolk, Virginia. Feeling muddled from the pain medication she'd taken, Sia gingerly touched the huge shiner that ringed her eye, flinching at the pain. She'd looked at it in the washroom mirror before she'd fallen asleep. "Yes, thank you."

The flight attendant left to get the water.

It seemed Sia could not get away from the man who haunted her, even in her sleep. All they had shared, gone in a matter of minutes. She didn't want to think about him. What they had shared was over in the time it took for a fighter jet to break apart and plummet to earth.

The flight attendant returned with the water. Forcing her thoughts back to the *James McCloud* and the now-deceased Master Chief Steven Walker, Sia took a sip of the cool liquid.

Sia's investigation had ended when Walker had gone over the side of the sponson, but she hadn't been able to find the bottle and the ME still hadn't finished the autopsy on Lieutenant Saunders. She was left with unanswered questions in both accidents. Additional statements from the crew confirmed a volatile relationship between the pilot and the master chief. Case closed.

Except Walker's words wouldn't stop eating at her. *Nope. Not saying it.* Did he have something to do with the accident that had taken her brother's life, or was he simply cruel? And what was he talking about when he cited duty as his reason for killing her?

She landed in Virginia at 1700 and intended to go home, take a long soak in the tub and sleep for twelve hours straight. But just as she pulled up to her apartment, her cell chimed and she was ordered to report to the JAG office on Naval Base Norfolk. The crisp March sky, an intense cobalt blue, and the barren trees hinting at a spring that was only weeks away did nothing to invigorate her.

At headquarters, the day was just ending. Sia was greeted by departing coworkers who first were concerned about her injuries, then ribbed her about going the wrong way. As she made her way down the hall, she saw one of her closest friends approaching. Special Agent Hollis McIntyre was one of the Naval Criminal Investigative Service's finest members. She was tough, smart and beautiful. The smile on her face changed to deep concern as they met.

"What the hell happened to you?" Hollis said as she took in Sia's bruises and her arm in the sling.

"It's a long story, one that will take several glasses of wine to tell." Hollis didn't know anything about her family or her brother's death. It was time she confided in her.

"Well, I hope the other guy got what was coming to him." Hollis sent her fist into her palm.

Sia nodded. "He did, but he left more questions than answers."

"Sounds like a thoroughly dangerous and frustrating TAD." Hollis touched Sia's good shoulder, giving her a squeeze.

"It was. Hence the need for wine."

Hollis laughed, but her eyes were still serious. She gave Sia a sympathetic and solemn look and said softly, "I'm so glad you're okay."

Sia nodded and smiled at her friend. "What brings you to JAG?"

Hollis rubbed at her tired-looking face. Her curly blond hair was more messy than usual. "A dead seaman and the guy we caught who did it. Just tying up some loose ends. I'm heading home. Why aren't you?"

Sia smiled wryly. "Boss calls and I answer like a dutiful soldier against injustice."

Hollis laughed. "When can we get those glasses of wine and catch up?"

"I'll give you a call when I'm finished here. Good?"

"Yes. That will give me a chance to go home, shower and change. Been on this case too long and it's starting to…ah…get rank."

Waving goodbye to Hollis, Sia entered the office

space where all the junior grade and clerical staff sat. Around them were the offices of the JAG team. She stopped at the desk of her aide, Legalman First Class Gabriel McBride, a young petty officer from Seattle.

"Commander Soto, welcome back. I've already printed out the report you sent me, and it's ready for the captain's review." He handed her a folder.

"McBride, you are a wonder."

He studied her face and winced. "Ouch on the shiner. Are you all right?"

"You should see the other guy. He took a header off the carrier. So I feel lucky to be alive."

"I'm sure glad you are, ma'am. It would be hard to train up a new boss."

She smiled. "Thanks for your concern." He smiled back and nodded. "McBride, I need for you to do some research for me on Master Chief Steven Walker. I want to know where he was stationed. Cross-reference his stations with any pilot accidents at the time he was serving those stations."

"Yes, ma'am."

After leaving her legalman, she made her way directly to her CO's office, receiving a wave through by his aide.

Entering, she saw Captain Mark Snyder was on the phone behind his desk. The look on his face was less than welcoming, but still he motioned her forward. He finished the conversation with clipped tones and hung up the phone.

Captain Snyder was a tall man, which was evident even when he was seated, as he was now. African-American with close-cropped hair, a wide nose and dark, piercing eyes, he cut an impressive figure in his blue coat and white shirt. As a commanding officer he was fair but tough and often liked to debate with her. "That was the skipper on the *U.S.S. James McCloud*."

Sia came to attention in front of his desk. When he nodded, she stood at ease, reached forward and placed the report on his desk. "Here's the final report on Walker...."

"This particular conversation doesn't have anything to do with the master chief," his voice was low and urgent.

"No?"

"They just had a pilot crash into the deck of the carrier."

"Oh, my God." Sia's heart lurched in her chest and she could see from the captain's grave look there was more. He motioned for her to sit and she sank into the nearest chair.

"Yes, Commander. It's even worse than that. He's Senator Mark Washington's son."

Her commander stared grimly at her, and Sia tried not to flinch. Her boss didn't assign blame. He wasn't petty and he treated her with respect. But at this moment, she saw the unmistakable truth in his eyes. He thought somehow she had let him down. A sick feeling churned in her stomach and squirmed up her spine.

"Send me back to the *McCloud* and I'll make sure I get to the bottom of this."

"It's not that easy, Commander Soto." He leaned back in his chair and sighed. "You are under investigation."

"Yes, it's a matter of routine. I understand, sir. But

I can still perform my duties and cooperate with any type of inquiry."

"I have no doubt of that. You are a meticulous investigator and litigator. But, this time, it's required you have help."

"Help? I don't need…"

Just then the door opened and her boss smiled. "Too late. He's already here."

She twisted around to take a look at the person who was going to accompany her on this assignment.

The pressure in the office changed, condensed. The man was six feet of raw energy in a tightly muscled package. He wore black pants that fit snugly against hard-packed thighs and a trim waist. A gray sweater stretched across his broad chest, with the edge of a plain white T-shirt at his strong throat. Over the sweater, he wore a black leather jacket. Clipped to his belt was the gold NCIS badge. The telltale bulge on the other side indicated he was carrying a sidearm. His thick black hair covered his forehead, errant tendrils curling along the nape of his neck.

Sia gasped as she looked into steady, beautiful dark gray eyes, eyes that had gazed into hers full of a smoky passion that only made them darken.

Oh, damn.

Christophe "Chris" Vargas.

Her brother's wingman.

The very pilot who had been directly responsible for her brother's death.

Chapter 2

Sia looked from her commanding officer to Chris, dumbfounded. It couldn't be. She was suddenly thrust back in time and all the longing, the desire and the need for this man came crashing into her.

It had been the wildest time of her life. He'd been a great fantasy, all hormones and hazard, and she'd been so crazy about him. He had been the only man her father had approved of, saying Chris was a first-rate pilot and the kind of man her father could trust.

Her father's approval had been important. With her father's consent came admiration. A man who could gain the trust and high regard of her father was worth her time.

Captain Snyder cleared his throat.

"Lieutenant Commander Ambrosia Soto, meet Special Agent Chris Vargas."

For a moment Sia's vocal cords wouldn't work, but she was saved from a response by Chris.

"Commander Soto and I are acquainted."

There were layers of meaning in his voice, a tone that touched her deep down and squeezed her heart. So much regret, pain and apology. Her eyes never just met Chris's—they connected like two live wires throwing off sparks. She could see by the look on his face he was studying her bruises and his mouth hardened. Her first thought was it was a good thing Master Chief Walker was dead. Chris's eyes, like polished steel, narrowed.

"Special Agent Vargas comes highly recommended from the director of NCIS," Captain Snyder said. "We're damn lucky to have him."

"Aye, sir," Sia responded. Chris never did anything by half. Sia had had no idea he'd left the Navy and gone into law enforcement. She'd assumed he was still flying.

The way Captain Snyder looked at her, Sia felt adrenaline release into her stomach. The message was loud and clear. Cooperate, don't make waves.

"Special Agent Vargas will take point on this, Commander."

"But it's my case. I'm the one…"

At the look from Captain Snyder, Sia closed her mouth on the words she was going to say. First off, he wouldn't be pleased she would in any way say she'd made a mistake. JAG didn't make mistakes. Second, she'd be usurping his authority. She was often able to get away with it because she was very good at verbal debate. But this time she saw he would yank her off this case in a heartbeat, and she would never get the answers she sought.

She stepped back and came to attention next to Chris. The first scent of him brought back memories of hot skin and heated kisses. She violently pushed those memories away, a resentment building.

Captain Snyder set the folder aside and addressed them both. "You're going back to the *U.S.S. James McCloud*, Commander Soto, and Special Agent Vargas will accompany you. You will look into the death of Senator Washington's son. Special Agent Vargas will be in charge."

"We need to get on a plane as soon as possible, sir," Chris said.

The captain picked up the phone. "That's taken care of. I suggest you get yourselves ready to go. I want daily reports."

"Captain, may I have a word with you? In private?" She glanced over at Chris and he smiled wryly. The protesting tone of her voice made her wince inside. She regretted her blunder immediately.

Captain Snyder sighed. "You're dismissed, Special Agent Vargas."

Chris gave her a sidelong look, but said nothing as he turned and left the office.

When the door was fully closed, Captain Snyder said, "Problem, Commander?"

"I have a history with Special Agent Vargas. It's complicated."

"Uncomplicate it and get the job done. Personal problems don't interest me. Results do. Although you are forcing me to rethink my decision to send you back to the *McCloud*."

"I can handle this assignment," she said quickly, immediately concerned the tenuous connection between Walker and her brother could snap if she wasn't given an opportunity to continue the investigation. "I don't need an NCIS agent breathing down my neck, dredging up old memories." Damn, she hadn't meant to say that. "I'm fully capable."

His eyes cooled. "I know you are capable. But protocol requires it and I'm not going to take a misstep here with the senator's son. You are still under investigation yourself."

"It's a routine investigation." She added "sir" when his eyes went glacial.

"I'm sure you wouldn't want this mishap to mar your record. This is going to be media fodder. I want it put to bed quickly."

Sia clenched her teeth. "Aye, sir."

Exiting the Captain's office, Sia looked for Chris and found him a few feet away. She walked up to him, grabbed him by his jacket and pulled him into an empty conference room. "You could have given me some kind of warning."

"I didn't know you were stationed here. Not until I walked into the Captain's office."

She didn't deserve this twist of fate. Of all the places he could have ended up, it had to be Norfolk. "I don't think it's a good idea we work together."

He shrugged. "It's easy. Work with me or Captain Snyder will assign someone else. Sounds like an easy choice to me."

Sia stared at Chris for several seconds, caught completely off guard again by his presence. After that debacle at her brother's grave site, she hadn't expected to see him ever again. Therefore, she'd had no chance to prepare herself to speak to him after what had happened six years ago. She had strategies filed away in her brain for every kind of courtroom situation, but she had no strategies for dealing with Chris and their short-lived, mind-blowing relationship.

"I don't want to work with you. You know perfectly well why." She wanted—no, needed—him to go away. She desperately needed to sort out her thoughts, and she couldn't do that with him standing less than five feet away, pinning her with that intent gaze of his. Maybe it was better not to confront him so directly. After all, it had been a while since she'd seen him. "Listen," she went on, trying to sound conciliatory, "I don't mean to sound like a bitch, really, I don't. It's just…it's been a very long day, and I'm not really prepared to deal with this *or you* at the moment."

Given her continued, rather visceral reaction to him, even after all these years, perhaps she'd never be ready to deal with him.

"I'm sure it has been a long day. And, yes, I know perfectly well why. Doesn't change a damn thing. Still your choice."

"I can't walk away from this. I want you to."

He shook his head, his gaze resolute. "Not going to happen. I don't answer to you or Captain Snyder, and I sure as hell don't answer to the Navy anymore. This is about Lieutenant Eli Washington."

"Don't lecture me. I know what it's about."

His eyes flared at her terse tone. "Just assign some-one else."

"I can't!" She clenched her fists, her outburst startling even her.

"Yes, you can. You just want to strong-arm me. It's always about your precious control. Well, I'm on this case, so get used to it."

It certainly had everything to do with control now. She'd given up her control to him six years ago. Fallen into such passion and heat, she'd barely been able to remember her name. Now standing so close to him, she felt the same damn pull, so overwhelming, so uncontrollable. He looked like the jets he used to fly: sleek, fast and dangerous.

He smelled way too good, musky and male, a combination as potent as a stiff belt of whiskey straight into the bloodstream. But she couldn't back up now and show any weakness. Chris would know he had the upper hand and that wouldn't be a good thing.

She laid it out bluntly, not seeing any reason to sugarcoat anything. "You're being stubborn because of what happened in our past. Is this payback, Chris?"

His face hardened. "Either do your job or pass it on to someone else, Commander Soto."

He hadn't taken the bait, and Sia realized she wasn't going to make him angry enough to walk away from the investigation. "I intend to do my job. Just without you involved."

He laughed then, without mirth. "It would be in your best interest to let someone else handle it."

She stiffened at his chiding tone. "You're alluding to the investigation into Master Chief Steven Walker's death?"

He folded his arms across his chest, the movement

tightening up his chest muscles and arms, pulling the jacket away from the gun clipped to his waist. "The Navy doesn't just casually investigate someone. You're the one who is under scrutiny."

"At the time I handled the investigation, I did it as thoroughly and diligently as I normally do." But in the back of her mind doubts assailed her. What if she had been too distracted by past memories and the fresh mourning of her brother's death? What if she had missed something?

"Is that where you got those bruises? Why your arm is in a sling?"

"Yes. Walker tried to kill me."

He shook his head. "Stupid man. What happened?"

"He took a header over the sponson and died from the fall. They fished his body up just after he went over."

"Really, in that vast of an ocean late at night?"

"He was wearing a life vest. A vest he denied me because I was supposed to be the one dead."

"Let me guess. They didn't find any evidence you helped him over?"

Weary from the day's events, she walked to the conference table and settled into one of the chairs. "No, because I dodged his attempt to throw me over. My hands were tied. It's the biggest indication the events happened exactly as I said they did. I didn't tie my own hands or wrench my own shoulder or give myself this black eye. The investigation is really just routine and to close the loop." She thrust out her good hand and showed him the bruises on her wrist.

He walked over and set his backside on the conference table. Taking her hand gently in his, he studied the black-and-blue marks. "That may be true, but it's the difference between us now. You have to follow the Navy's rules. I don't."

His hand was warm, his palm smooth. Her heart fluttering, she pulled her hand from his hold. "Surely in your job you're required to follow rules."

He smiled. "When it suits me, but as a civilian investigator, I have a lot more leeway than you do."

The smile lighting up his eyes made her remember the potency he wielded with his irresistible charm, all the more reason not to work with him. The other big reason was he'd been directly responsible for her brother's death and the destruction of her family.

It was as if he'd been waiting for her to think that very thought. His eyes changed, got a little harder, a little darker. "I didn't come here to dredge up the past, Sia."

"It doesn't matter whether you talk about it or not. Just seeing you brings it all back."

His mouth tightened and he looked away from her. "I'm sorry for that."

"You said you were sorry six years ago when they handed my mother his flag. It still doesn't help."

He closed his eyes, but not before she saw the flash of pain and, suddenly, she felt sick for the way everything had ended.

"You're not the only one who suffered, Sia. I lost you and your brother. I have to live with what I did to him, to you."

She felt a distinct tug on her heart, but refused to examine it too closely. Yet she did finally give into the urge to reach out and touch his arm, needing that physical contact in a soul-deep way. The leather was warm from his body heat, the muscles beneath taut and corded. "I can't help the way I feel about it, Chris."

"I know you can't, but that doesn't make it any easier to forget what we had. What we shared." He covered her hand with his, the warmth comforting.

"What we have to deal with now is the present. We can't change the past."

"No, we can't," he whispered. "There's no place for us to go at all."

"Don't," she protested.

The warning was diluted to nothing by the sadness in his face. His mouth twisted into a half smile that was cynical and weary. His dark eyes looked a hundred years old.

Even surrounded by family and friends, she'd been so alone when her brother had died. All she'd wanted, longed for, was to have Chris hold her. But the grief of her brother's death tripled when she'd found out Chris had caused the accident. He would never hold her again.

Dangerous, her longing and his proximity.

A quick knock on the door made her sit up straight and release him. She rose, walked to the door and opened it. Her aide was on the other side.

"Excuse me, Commander Soto, Captain Snyder's aide pointed me in this direction. I was able to get you and Agent Vargas on a flight to Hawaii via L.A. The *McCloud* is currently docked at Pearl for repairs to the flight deck. Your flight leaves in three hours. He handed her a folder, giving Chris the once-over. "Your e-tickets are in there."

"Thank you, McBride."

He seemed reluctant to leave her alone. Her legal-man eyed Chris and his gaze returned to Sia. "Can I escort you to your car?"

"No, that won't be necessary. Good night, McBride."

Chris smiled wryly as the petty officer deliberately left the door open. "He's looking at me like I'm a psycho, serial killer."

"You look formidable, that's all. McBride doesn't know you."

"No, he doesn't."

She sighed. "You're not going to change your mind."

"Hell, no." He made his way to the open door and passed her. "Why don't you let this investigation go, Sia?"

"I might have missed something. Something important!" Her voice was loud in the small room. Softer, she said, "I have to fix it or make sure my conclusions were sound. If I neglected to fully handle this investigation and I caused a man's death…"

He stepped up to her until he was close. "I hear you're expected to get over that, too," he said softly.

Her throat ached with the pain in his voice.

"We have to work together. I'll accept that. But don't expect anything else from me," she said, delivering the ultimatum with a tone that accepted her defeat.

Even as the words left her mouth, she knew she was even more than ten times a fool if she believed either of them could forget the fire between them whenever they touched, or looked at each other, or were in the same damn room.

Chris said absolutely nothing. Out of everything that had happened to her in the past twenty-four hours, his silence was more nerve-racking than waiting for a verdict. His silence was downright ominous.

She was in trouble. Oh, man, was she in trouble, but she wasn't going to give in to panic. Later she could panic, but not now while she was standing in front of him. She needed her wits.

Dredging up old memories wasn't conducive to this situation. But it seemed wits and good sense deserted her when he turned those dark eyes on her, when he looked at her as if she were the most desirable, most important woman on earth. She tried to break the spell by thinking Chris probably looked at every woman he wanted that way, but the thought seemed to slip out of her mind like smoke.

Finally he spoke. "I don't have any expectations where you are concerned. I learned that valuable lesson six years ago." His tone was accusing and his eyes brooked no disagreement. It was clear he was disgusted with her lack of support at the grave site. She was smart enough to keep quiet about that.

His face was too close to hers and she couldn't stop herself from thinking about him kissing her. And her mouth ached, waiting a beat, then two, the tension drawing as tight as a wire. Finally he pulled away, turned on his heel and exited the conference room.

It was a while before Sia could make her limbs move.

Oh, yes, she was in deep trouble.

Finally her training slammed into place and she was able to get herself under control.

She needed to get a grip on her emotions—a highly unlikely occurrence when she was still using everything she had not to remember how it was to melt into Chris's arms.

The temptation of him whispered across her exposed skin. These feelings and sensations only made her more resolved not to give in. Her brother was no longer alive because of Chris. She had to remember that information, use it to keep her own emotions from eating her alive.

A little doubt wiggled its way in when she remembered the words of the master chief. Could he have done something to Chris and caused the accident that killed her brother? If he had, then maybe Chris would be exonerated right along with her brother.

And if Chris wasn't guilty of causing the accident that killed her brother, then maybe…

She was jumping the gun here. That was a big if. At this point, she had to keep her distance. She had an investigation to handle. Her baggage with Chris couldn't get in the way of that.

Straightening her uniform jacket, she pushed open the conference-room door and exited, trying to push away the feeling that disaster loomed right around the corner.

Chris stalked out of JAG. Immediately a woman pushed a microphone into his face.

"Agent Vargas. Can you give us any information regarding the death of Senator Washington's son?"

"No comment," he growled and ignored the attempts of the other reporters to get his attention. He pushed the button on his key ring to unlock his car. When he got inside, he slammed the door. Even after all these years, it felt as if they had never been apart.

Shutting out the loud calls of the reporters around the driver's side of his car, his thoughts went back to Sia. He had thought he knew what he would say to Sia when he saw her again. His eyes burned remembering the day of the crash and her face when they'd told her Rafael was dead. He'd never forget the way she'd looked at him. It was shortly afterward that the trembling started every time he sat in a cockpit. It was that look that ultimately forced him to hang up his wings. He'd survived. By sheer luck, he was still standing. But inside he was dying.

After completing his Top Gun training, Chris had been assigned to the *U.S.S. James McCloud* and there met his new wingman, Lieutenant Rafael Soto. Chris was high on his success, his ability to make it to the top of his class. He had his afterburner on and he was flying right into the sun, pulling G's.

He'd shown his father he wasn't good for nothing. Then everything came crashing down.

A sharp rap on the window brought him back to himself. He started his car and drove away without even a glance at the reporters.

Chris had worked with Rafael for two years before he'd met Sia. The *James McCloud* had docked in Norfolk and Rafael had invited Chris to a family gathering. Rafael had been like the brother Chris never had. He was an ace in the air, his knowledge and abilities impressive. He made Chris want to work harder to keep up.

The night he'd met Sia, Chris was cocky and full of himself as only a pilot can be. Feeling he was finally slipping into a family situation he'd always dreamed of, he'd thought Sia would make a fine sister. Then he'd seen her, and any brotherly feelings dissipated in the wake of her sheer effect on him.

Long, coffee-rich hair, dark sensual eyes, and a no-holds-barred attitude only made him want to subdue her in the most carnal way. He took one look at her and knew what would happen between them was inevitable.

She had a knockout, head-turning shape that made the blood in his veins sizzle. But more than her physical appearance attracted him. The minute she opened her mouth and began to spar with him verbally, well, that was the kicker.

Whenever he was stressed, he would revert back to those days when he was on top of the world and seducing Sia had been as natural as breathing. Their first time together still burned in his brain and remained imprinted on his heart.

Chris reached his apartment and was soon out of his car and in his bedroom. Pulling a suitcase from his closet, he started packing.

NCIS had sustained him through the loss of Rafael. But underlying that grief was the agony of losing Sia. Nothing and no one could alleviate that gut-wrenching pain. No one but Sia. He guessed that wasn't the top priority on her list of things to do.

He was on his own, as he'd been most of his life—a reality that had become painfully clear to him after Rafael had died.

Suddenly he stopped packing and straightened, swallowing hard at the memories that flooded over him.

He and Sia had been wrapped up in each other that

summer. With her diploma from Yale, she had easily snagged a prestigious job at a law firm in New York City. Her job was slated to begin in the fall, but they had made plans to be together. Sia was going to break the news to her father that she couldn't go to New York. She loved Chris and wanted to stay in Norfolk.

They had planned a life together and Sia had been so in love with him…until…the accident.

That's when everything had changed. Sia had abandoned him when he'd needed her the most. She'd sided with her family and cut him out of her life as if he meant nothing. For him it had been the ultimate betrayal.

And Chris had lost everything that mattered.

Hollis removed Sia's uniforms from the dryer and walked to her kitchen table, setting them down.

"Here I thought we'd be chugging wine, not doing domestic chores."

"I'm sorry, but I've got to get back on a plane in two hours and then on to Pearl. I appreciate you helping me. This shoulder is still pretty sore and I'm supposed to rest it for another day at least."

"Ah, the glamorous life of a JAG officer."

Sia snorted. "Right."

Hollis gave her a sidelong glance. "What's wrong? You look…unsettled."

"You know what? To hell with it." Sia walked to her kitchen cabinet and pulled out two wineglasses. Hollis smiled, stopped fussing with Sia's uniforms and walked over. "I've neglected to tell you about someone from my past."

"Oh, does this someone have to do with that unsettled look I mentioned?"

Sia pulled a bottle of Riesling out of the fridge and popped the cork, pouring a generous amount into each glass. "He does. I have to work with him and I have to take orders from him. I think it might be someone you know."

"Really? Who?" Hollis took a sip of her wine.

"Special Agent Chris Vargas."

"Chris? You were once up close and personal with Chris Vargas? Oh my, he is a hottie. All the female agents drool over him."

"Including you?"

"Well, come on, he's gorgeous and I'm female."

Sia took a sip of her wine, her emotions ragged. "We have a painful past, Hollis, and I'm not sure how I'm going to work with him."

"Oh, sweetie, I'm sorry to trivialize your feelings." She took Sia's arm and led her over to the table. Settling in her seat, Hollis set her wineglass down and reached for a uniform shirt and a hanger. "Okay, spill."

Sia told Hollis everything. Afterward, Hollis was quiet for a moment, then in one swallow she finished off her wine. "I can only respond in one way. Chris is a decent guy and a top-notch agent. You couldn't have a better partner out there watching your back."

After Hollis left and Sia was driving to the airport, she felt even more uncomfortable with the situation. Sia trusted Hollis, and her observations of people were always accurate. It unsettled Sia to think that all those years ago, she might have been so mired in her grief that she'd unfairly judged Chris.

Chapter 3

It was easy to pick Sia out of a crowd. It was true being in Navy service khaki helped her to stand out, and it was also true she had her arm in a sling and had a very dark black eye compliments of a dead master chief. But it wasn't any of those things that made her easy to find.

Sia commanded attention, she moved and breathed confidence. Her dark hair was ruthlessly pulled back, her Navy cap situated firmly under her arm.

She also had a long line of reporters dogging her steps, but she said nothing to them as she approached.

He had no illusions he would get a welcoming smile. She'd made it quite clear she didn't want him on this case, but that was too bad. He should have turned this assignment over to another agent, but he couldn't. Whether it was to be contrary or something else, he didn't know. From the look on her face, it was clear she was still royally pissed off at him.

He was okay with that. Seeing her had stirred pain and regret, but it had also stirred emotions he had long forgotten. How he had loved this woman. His chest still ached with it; his body still yearned for her.

"All set?" he asked as the same woman from last night tried to once again get his attention. "No comment," he replied.

Her mouth tightened as she asked him another question he blatantly ignored.

Sia gave him a curt nod, and they headed for the security checkpoint. As soon as they reached the staging area, he showed his badge to the official and indicated the sidearm at his waist. The official checked all his papers and then Sia's, as well.

"You're not carrying a firearm, ma'am?" the TSA official asked.

Sia smiled. "No, I'm a lawyer. The only deadly things I carry are my mind for litigation and my very loaded briefcase."

The official laughed, and they were allowed to pass. Thankfully the reporters were left behind, but Chris was sure there would be a fresh batch when they landed. Once in the gate area, it wasn't long before the plane was scheduled to take off. Once on board and securely buckled in, Sia sipped at a cup of coffee she'd purchased and remained silent.

After stowing his own gear, Chris settled himself into his seat. Buckling his seat belt, he glanced over at her. She stared resolutely ahead and it irked him. Surely they couldn't sit in silence for the whole flight. He knew that would suit her, but it didn't suit him. "How did you end up at JAG?"

She turned to look at him, taking another sip of her coffee. He accepted her cool look with one of his own. Although she was as impeccably groomed as ever, there was a hint of strain around her mouth that had only intensified since he'd last seen her. The thought occurred to him she worked too hard, but then he did, too. It was mandatory to keep the ghosts at bay. It was certainly better than drinking himself to death. After Rafael died and Sia withdrew from him, he'd tried that route and discarded it as a coward's way out.

"I applied shortly after Rafael was killed." Her tone was clipped and didn't invite him to ask any more questions, but of course that wasn't going to stop him.

"Why?"

"Why?" she repeated through clenched teeth.

"Yes. Why did you join JAG?"

She huffed out a breath. "It was a way to carry on what he had wanted to do in the Navy—serve his country. I'm not a pilot so I served in the only capacity I knew—the law."

"Did they send you to Newport?"

She turned to look at him with a steady gaze. "Are we playing twenty questions? That could work both ways."

"I'm only trying to find out what happened to you after we parted. I'm curious."

As a cop he was adept at reading body language. He noticed she didn't turn hers toward him as one would do in an intimate conversation. Sia was setting the boundaries, and it seemed they were impenetrable.

"Yes, I went to Newport, Rhode Island, and completed Naval Justice School after I finished Officer Development School."

"You sound like you're reciting your name, rank and serial number. I'm not the enemy."

"We may be on the same side, but that is as far as it goes. You refused to cooperate with me and you are in charge of an investigation that should have been mine. So excuse me for thinking of you as the enemy. Besides, I'm only relating the information you wanted, Special Agent Vargas."

"And you got to pick where you wanted to go?"

She sighed, but when he made it clear by his look he wasn't going to give up, she answered. "Yes, I did."

He smiled now.

Sia frowned. "What's so funny?"

"You're just answering the question."

Her eyes, steamed to a volatile brown, regarded him with pique. "Isn't that what I'm supposed to do?" When she spoke, her tone gave no indication of how she felt about his unwanted questions. Still the cool cucumber. With her dark hair pulled back, not so much as a dab of makeup enhancing her smooth-as-silk skin, and her crisp and unwrinkled uniform ruthlessly fit to her small frame, she was every inch the woman in control.

He ran his fingers through his longish hair. He should have had it cut weeks ago, but his caseload had been brutal. It was a mechanism to keep himself from reaching for her to see if he could muss up that too-perfect control a little. "You're being deliberately obtuse and you know it."

"Oh. You want me to elaborate like we're old friends," she said, but her casual tone was belied by a quick swallow, and the way her hands flexed in her lap. "We're not old friends."

"I know that. But I thought since we're going to be together for a while it might be a good idea to get re-acquainted."

"I think I made myself clear yesterday. We're working together because you forced the issue. Doesn't mean I have to cooperate or make small talk."

"No, it doesn't, but I want you to indulge me."

"If I don't, will you make a report of it to Captain Snyder in the vein of, 'Commander Soto is a competent investigator but she won't indulge me in small talk'? Oh, no. I'll have that on my record. How will I live it down?"

She frustrated him to the extreme—in ways he remembered and, surprisingly, cherished. All she had to do was look at him in a certain way and there it was. It was why he reacted to her in this crazy way when there was even a hint of banter.

He should have given in to her request to let someone else at NCIS accompany her to the carrier. Handling his caseload was enough without this long-term temporary assignment. Chasing Navy and Marine Corps killers, thieves and criminals was a full-time job and then some, but it was preferable to dealing with all this inner turmoil. He'd spent the last six years trying to forget Sia. It should be telling he hadn't been able to do it and he was right back where he started.

She wasn't looking at him, and her tone was flat and hard. But he saw the tremor in her jaw, the vein standing out in stark relief along the side of her creamy neck, and the white knuckles as she gripped the armrest of her seat.

"I know how you feel about me being here, but you better suck it up like a good sailor. I'm going to lead this investigation and make sure it's done right. I have the experience and I have the authority. Hell, you should be grateful for my help and a second pair of eyes on this whole mess."

Her cheeks drained of color and she swallowed hard.

"You almost died the last time you were on the *Mc-Cloud,* and I will do everything in my power to see you're never put in that position again. So, stop being so damn stubborn and release your backbone a bit."

Her chest rose and fell more quickly.

"Look at me."

Her throat worked.

"Sia."

She swung her gaze to his, and there was no mistaking the fatigue, the wariness and the healthy dose of anger he saw there. "What?"

"To be perfectly honest, I believe if not for these whacked-out circumstances, we would have never set eyes on each other again. But we have. That may give us a chance to finally put the past behind us and move on. Seeing you again has stirred up a bunch of stuff I thought I was long done with."

She looked away, blinking rapidly.

He dropped his gaze, the emotion building in his chest. Oh, damn, please don't let her cry.

He felt her gaze flicker to his and looked up in time to catch it, hold it. He saw her overcome her emotions and get herself under control. Ah, yes, Sia was certainly made of sterner stuff. If she let herself go, just once, maybe she could learn it was okay to be vulnerable, to lean.

"I think you are mistaken, Agent Vargas. I have put you and what happened in the past. I think you're the one who needs something more. I suggest you get over it because I have no interest in dredging it up. What we had got destroyed."

"Did it?" He held her gaze for a few heartbeats as the color seeped back into her cheeks. "That remains to be seen."

"You didn't let me finish. It got destroyed by you. Now you can suck it up." She rose. "Excuse me. I have to go to the head."

He stood so she could pass, her body contacting with his all the way from his chest to his knees. The plane hit some turbulence and Sia was thrown against him. He held on to her instinctively so she wouldn't fall onto her injured shoulder. The interior of the plane was dark; only the small overhead light on their panel was on. Most of the passengers had decided to sleep since the red-eye flight wouldn't get into L.A. until early morning.

Once the turbulence passed, he didn't let her go. They stared at each other, her face close to his, her mouth soft and damp, glistening in the dimness. Their silence expanded in a way that lent texture to the very air between them. In the close quarters, the air was warm, with little ventilation. Her face was in shadows, but the dim light only outlined her beautiful bone structure, her startled eyes that had green and gold flecks in the deep brown.

"Thank you for not letting me fall," she said softly, her voice cracking, showing how unsettled she was.

He let her go as she pushed at him with her good arm. As she disappeared down the passageway, he had a hard time tamping down his own roiling emotions.

No matter what she said, her feelings weren't in the past. Far from it.

He didn't let himself hope. That would have been foolish, but he did crack the door to perhaps let in hope, if it was so inclined to sneak in when he wasn't looking.

Sia leaned against the head's door. With a soft sound of protest she sank down onto the seat. She turned her head and looked at herself in the mirror. She squeezed her eyes shut, but it only made the images in her head starker, clearer.

Chris was potent at a distance, but close up…he was lethal. She felt the power in his hands as he'd gently supported her through the turbulence. His eyes were a window into his soul, straightforward, sincere and tough. He was all those things and more. How could she have forgotten how much he stirred her blood, how easily she could fall into those fathomless eyes, like descending into a mist that cast a magic spell over her.

She scrubbed at her face with her free hand. Her shoulder throbbed and her eye looked especially ugly with the purple-green-and-black bruise standing out starkly against her white skin.

All of her feelings for him rushed back and she couldn't control them. The pain at her memories of him, of making love to him, of being with him and living with him were more than precious to her, more than sacred. But she had to be smart. The memory of how she'd felt when she'd learned about her brother's death and Chris's pilot error that had allowed him to eject and her brother to die also came rushing back, warring with her need and regard for him.

She couldn't dredge this up, couldn't allow this to color her life or mess with her head. She had to stay focused and do the job she'd been sent to do and do it right.

"This time, I have to make sure it's right," she whispered, her voice breaking. "I have to."

Her shoulders slumped a tiny bit as she tried hard to fight off the inevitable reality check.

It didn't help that she was exhausted. She hadn't slept in twenty-four hours and now she was headed back to the carrier where she'd almost lost her life. Where the master chief had died trying to kill her.

She only wished she had thought to ask him the burning question that was now troubling her. Why? Why had he tried to kill her? What had she gotten close to or stumbled on to or would have stumbled on to if she'd been given the opportunity to question him and bring him up on charges? Had she taken a misstep and been blinded by her own emotions? Was she responsible for Lieutenant Washington's death? Could she even make this right at all?

All the answers were aboard the *U.S.S. James McCloud,* the ship of memories.

When she got back to her seat, she slipped past Chris as quickly and impersonally as she could. He didn't say anything and that suited her fine. She reached down for her purse and fumbled inside trying to find her pain-killer, but with one hand it was awkward.

Chris took her purse from her and reached inside and found the bottle. He popped open the top and handed her the tablets. Motioning for the flight attendant, he requested water for her.

Sia took the medication and leaned back in her seat.

"Get some rest," Chris whispered, reaching up to turn off the panel light. Sia closed her eyes and sighed as the medication started to do its work.

How was she supposed to shore up her defenses, re-sume her steely-eyed distance from a guy like Chris? Half of her wanted to fall into his lap right now.

She needed to get back to the no-nonsense woman she'd made herself into or she wouldn't have any hope of surviving the next few weeks with him and keeping her heart intact.

A prayer was on her tongue as she fell asleep, but she wasn't sure exactly what she was praying for.

The sound of the captain's voice and the dim lighting of the plane woke her with a start. She sighed dream-ily and snuggled deeper against the firm pillow, her hand reaching around a trim waist to come up against hard metal.

She opened her eyes to find her face pillowed against Chris's hard, muscled chest. His sleepy eyes regarded her with interest and something a drowsy Chris couldn't conceal. She jerked back and groaned softly at the pain in her shoulder and that look disappeared from his eyes. It made her feel almost sad about it, but knew it was better for her own equilibrium.

"Steady," he said softly. "No harm in resting comfortably and God knows that's tough to do on a plane."

Her awareness of him was as finely tuned as her senses were in the courtroom. Except with him, there was all that sexual energy jacking things up. She cleared her throat, maybe squared her shoulders a little, and then made the mistake of looking back at him before reaching for her purse.

Something about the morning beard shadowing his jaw, the way his dark hair was all mussed up, made his smoky eyes darker, and enhanced how impossibly thick his eyelashes were. His mouth looked way too sexy and kissable in the dim light.

She turned away and raised the shade on the window and saw LAX below her as they lined up with the runway to set down. The captain came back on the speaker to let everyone know the temperature and that they would be at the gate shortly.

As soon as the plane stopped, passengers were up reaching for their stowed luggage.

Chris rose, too, and Sia tried not to stare at the way his muscles flexed and elongated beneath his clothes as he reached up for their luggage. How his sweater went tight over his biceps or the way it made his shoulders look wider.

He dipped down and eyed her. "Are you ready? Do you need help?"

"No," she said quickly, not sure how she would handle having those powerful hands on her again. Let him think she was just a bit stiff and sleepy. More the better for her if Chris never knew the level of fascination she'd had for him. Still had, apparently. Dammit.

She reached down and grabbed her purse and briefcase. Rising, she moved out from the seats and slipped into the space in front of him.

She tried her best to appear unaffected and coolly in control as they deplaned. But Chris's long-legged stride kept him right at her back. And she could feel him there, just behind her, in a rather primal way that had the power to skew her internal equilibrium.

Chris took her arm when she headed for the escalator and directed her toward the elevator. He reached past her and pressed the button. When he stepped in after her, she felt a bit claustrophobic, as if he was suddenly taking up too much space, using up way too much of her precious air. And yet he was standing a respectable distance from her, not so much as looking at her. Which did nothing to stop her from thinking how satisfying it would be to push the emergency stop and caress his face, kiss that sexy mouth, watch his eyes heat.

It only made her mood swing to the nasty. "Afraid you wouldn't be able to hold my hand on the escalator like my mommy?"

"Yes," he simply said.

It only made her fume.

Then her stomach growled so loud it was audible above the din outside the slowly descending elevator.

"Sounds like you need something to eat, little girl."

She let his dig go with a perfectly sweet smile.

"Let's get some breakfast, then. We have two hours before our flight leaves."

"I can't hide the fact that I'm starving."

"When was the last time you ate?"

"I don't remember."

After breakfast, it was a short walk to the gate, then on to the flight. It wasn't long before they were touching down at the Honolulu airport, where they were picked up by a Navy car to take them to the *U.S.S. James Mc-Cloud*. A large crowd of reporters were only able to get in a few questions before Sia and Chris were tucked inside the vehicle.

At the sight of the ship and the sponsor in particular, a chill ran over Sia's skin. She could see where part of the flight deck had been scorched and that crews were working on the damaged area of the vessel.

The *U.S.S. James McCloud* was only one of a large fleet of carriers in the Navy. The flight deck, angled at nine degrees, which allowed aircraft to be launched and recovered simultaneously, took up the majority of the available space on the ship. The ship carried a full wing of 12/14 F/A-18F Super Hornets as strike fighters, another two squadrons of 10-12 F/A-18C Hornets, as well as early-warning aircraft, a helicopter and anti-submarine squadron. Each carrier-based aircraft used a tailhook bolted to an eight-foot bar that extended from the craft to catch one of four cables on the deck of the carrier. The cables were engineered to stop any aircraft at exactly the same spot on the deck no matter the size or weight of the craft.

The prominent bridge was situated to starboard, which Sia learned early on in her career was the right side of a ship.

Once on board, they were directed to the NCIS agent a-float, Clarissa Weston.

"Ahoy," she called out as they entered her office. "Chris! It's good to see you. I got word you and Commander Soto were coming aboard to investigate this tragedy. My office is at your command."

"Thanks, Clarissa. It's good to see you again. What do you have so far?"

"I'm sure you'll want to do your own investigations, Chris, but so far all I've done is make sure no one has left the ship. That went over big. Most of these people have been cooped up on this vessel for three months, but this port stop isn't for fun. It's to get repairs to the flight deck Lieutenant Washington tore up when he crash-landed." She turned to Sia. "It's good to see you again, ma'am. Wow, that's a nasty shiner. I sure hope you're healing okay."

"I'm doing fine, Clarissa. Thank you for asking."

"The legal office is also at your disposal, Chris, ma'am. Commander Stryker is expecting you."

"Thank you," Chris said.

"The captain asked that you report to him as soon as you were aboard. He's at Pri-Fly, the Primary Flight Control center. I'll take you to him now."

Sia was now familiar with the carrier after spending time on the ship during her investigation. They headed toward what was called the "island"—the command center for flight-deck operation as well as the ship as a whole. The island was about one hundred and fifty feet tall, but only twenty feet wide, so it wouldn't take up too much space on the flight deck.

The top of the island sported an array of radar and communications antennas, which kept tabs on surrounding ships and picked up satellite phone and TV signals. Below that was their destination, Pri-Fly. At the next level was the bridge, where the captain directed the helmsman who actually steered the carrier.

Sia clumsily navigated several ladders due to her injured shoulder as Clarissa ushered them into the Pri-Fly main area, where Captain Thaddeus Maddox was looking through a set of binoculars at the damaged part of the deck.

Without turning around, he said, "Commander Soto. I can't say I'm thrilled to have you back aboard my ship."

"Good morning, sir. Under the circumstances, I can't say I'm thrilled to be back." He was an intimidating man, with a strong, iron-hard jaw and salt-and-pepper hair. His posture was ramrod straight and he commanded the very air around him.

The captain set down the binoculars and turned around. He walked forward and nodded to Clarissa. "Thank you, Agent Weston."

She nodded and took her leave.

Chris reached out his hand. "Special Agent Chris Vargas, sir."

The captain shook his hand, but only briefly met Chris's eyes. He returned his gaze to Sia, and she stood at attention until the captain said, "At ease."

He turned to a stocky blond man standing next to him. "This is my XO, Commander Seth Tate. If I'm not available, you can speak to him."

He then addressed Sia. "Your report put the death of Lieutenant Malcolm Saunders directly on the master chief's shoulders. How do you explain what has happened with Lieutenant Washington?"

"I've only arrived, sir, and haven't had a chance to even review preliminary information."

The captain's eyes narrowed. "Well, I expect you will have answers for me, Commander Soto. I have another dead aviator, lost another expensive aircraft and have a damaged ship. I'm not happy."

"With all due respect, Skipper," Chris said, "I read Commander Soto's report and I would have drawn the same conclusions. She did a thorough investigation and on top of it almost lost her life. It was clear to her at the time she had the right suspect."

"I concede the investigation was thorough, Special Agent Vargas. I will give her that, and she did put her life at risk. But if this investigation into the senator's son's death turns up he was murdered, then it's obvious there was something more to the story than was evident at the time."

She wasn't supposed to go all warm inside when Chris stuck up for her. "Agreed, sir," Sia said. "But Special Agent Vargas is in charge. I answer to him."

"Noted," the captain said. "Stow your gear and get to work. We'll be leaving port in about a day or two. The needed repairs weren't major."

"Aye, sir," Sia said, coming to attention. She executed a perfect turn and left Pri-Fly with Chris following behind.

Back at Agent Weston's office, Clarissa volunteered to show Chris to his stateroom. Sia had been assigned the same stateroom as on her last visit. This time, though, her roommate had been transferred to another billet, which left Sia enjoying the stateroom all to herself. She only meant to lie down for a moment, but fell asleep. When she woke up, she saw she'd been asleep for a couple of hours. After freshening and changing her uniform, she was free to visit the legal office.

Commander William Stryker greeted her as she entered. "Hello, Sia. Sorry you had to come back here so soon."

"Me, too, Billy. What do you have so far?"

"Not much. I've done some preliminary questioning of personnel and I've compiled that into this file." He handed her a folder. "Agent Weston wanted me to pass the autopsy report for Lieutenant Saunders to you."

Sia opened it and quickly skimmed the contents. "Thanks. I'll read this later," she said and tucked it into her briefcase.

"I've also compiled a list of people who were directly responsible for the two jets and any other personnel who may have witnessed the accident." He handed her a sheaf of papers and Sia went to tuck them into the folder.

"Good work. That's what I'm looking for," Sia said.

Chris's deep, resonant voice stopped the action she was about to perform. "Don't you mean that's what *we're* looking for?"

She turned to find Chris standing in the doorway. "Commander William Stryker, this is the lead investigator, Special Agent Chris Vargas."

Billy nodded, eyeing Chris.

Chris came up to her and looked over her shoulder at the list in her hand. "Let's take the first name and make our way down the list."

Sia nodded.

Billy looked at the name at the top of the list. "Airman Trudy Schover. I'll get her in here for you."

It wasn't long before the woman was sitting across the same table where Sia had interrogated the master chief.

"Tell me where you were and what happened when Lieutenant Washington's F/A-18 crashed into the deck," Sia asked the young dark-haired woman. Her hands were clasped together in front of her and she was wringing them.

"I was in Pri-Fly handling the communication between the planes." She looked at Chris. "I'm like an air traffic controller."

"It's okay, Airman, I was a pilot." She acknowledged that with a nod of her head. "Did you know Lieutenant Washington?" Chris continued, leaning back and folding his arms across his chest.

Trudy shook her head, her eyes sincere. "No, sir. I didn't."

"Continue," Chris said.

"Everything went routinely and that night was clear as glass, no clouds in the sky. Lieutenants Washington and Monroe took off. About three minutes into the flight, Lieutenant Monroe yelled for Lieutenant Washington to get his nose up."

"Did Lieutenant Washington respond?" Chris leaned forward, his eyes intent.

"Yes, he said that he was having problems with his radar."

"His radar?" Chris asked, as he set his hands on the table and concentrated on the airman's words.

"Yes, sir. He said it was malfunctioning." Her voice strained, Trudy stopped talking, her eyes going unfocused. She was trying to remember.

"In what way?"

"Total failure. No instruments," she said solemnly.

"But he was trained to land without them, correct?" Sia asked. With each word her throat got tighter. She'd read her brother's report years after his death, and as Trudy related the incident, Sia became more alarmed.

"Yes, ma'am. I tried to initiate communication just before the crash. He had his nose down. Lieutenant Monroe was yelling at him to bring his nose up and the flight crew handling the meatball were waving him off, but it was too late. He hit the deck hard, skidded across the platform and right off the end of the carrier, exploding as he dropped into the sea." Her voice broke and held a note of the shock she still seemed to be experiencing, her eyes moist.

"He didn't even attempt to eject?" Chris asked.

"No, sir."

"Meatball?" Sia said looking at the airman for an explanation.

"It's a series of lights that are calibrated to the horizon. It serves as a safeguard when pilots are landing on the carrier. If a pilot sees green, safe to land, if red, they need to break off and circle around to land again. The circles of light look like meatballs, so that's how it got its name."

"Any other observations, Airman?" Chris asked.

"Only that he was one of the finest pilots I've ever worked with," she said emphatically. "I didn't know him personally, but I knew him as a pilot. I was shocked to see his nose down like that. It was worse than a rookie mistake, malfunction or not."

"Thank you, Airman," Chris said.

Trudy nodded, but before she left, she turned back, tear tracks down her cheeks. "I hope you clear him of any blame. He doesn't deserve to have his record marred this way."

All Sia could offer her was a quick nod, her emotions in turmoil and thoughts of her brother foremost in her thoughts.

When the door closed behind Airman Schover, Chris turned to Sia. "Sounds like he could have made a mistake with the radar off. But he would have noticed if the meatball lights were red."

"Maybe he was impaired. He could have been too short on oxygen, or some other explanation."

Chris took a deep breath and then released it slowly. "That's exactly how it went down when Rafael died, only my plane was still in the air and I ejected."

Silence filled the compartment, the kind that wove around the heart and squeezed tight.

Chapter 4

Just the mention of her brother's name made Sia remember him and the day he'd died. She'd been figuring out the best way to tell her father she wasn't going to New York. She wasn't going to take a job that was too far away from Chris.

She had answered the door when the Navy had come knocking to break the news about her brother. At first, she thought they had come to tell her Chris was dead and her heart had throbbed painfully in her chest. But when they'd told her it was her brother, the guilt only mixed in with the terrible grief and relief it hadn't been Chris.

She could tell by looking at Chris he was remembering that day, too. His beard-shadowed jaw hardened and his eyes went distant.

"Do you think we're dealing with more than pilot error in all these incidents?" she asked him, watching as his eyes focused again, but the pain and the grief lingered in their depths.

"I don't want to jump to conclusions, but my gut is telling me something. I don't usually ignore it."

She turned away from the emotion that darkened his eyes and set his mouth in a grim line. "What is your gut telling you?" The lack of sleep, the quick trip to Pearl and her injuries were beginning to take a toll. She leaned back in her chair and rubbed at her tired face.

Chris didn't miss the movement and his intense eyes studied her. "That somehow, some way, the two incidents might be connected."

For an instant her heart stopped. Now it was racing. "Do you remember Master Chief Walker from the *McCloud* six years ago?"

Chris shook his head. "The people who serviced the planes were never really on my radar. I lived to fly and my focus was always on that. When Rafael and I hit the cockpits, we flew for the Navy, but it was pure joy. It's tragedy enough to lose one pilot, but two in such a short span of time is…suspect." His voice was reflective and sad. The sound of it squeezed her heart.

She was finding sympathy in all the tragedy. She was feeling some of the guilt that Chris must have felt when her brother's plane had been destroyed. Although she had no emotional ties to Lieutenant Washington, she regretted any action that she hadn't taken to ensure that no more deaths attributed to Master Chief Walker occurred. Then she realized the truth. It couldn't have been Walker. He was dead. What did that mean?

"Oh, damn, there's one flaw in our suspicions." She

folded her arms and tucked herself back into her seat, some of her doubts beginning to surface.

Chris held her gaze. "What is that?"

"Master Chief Walker died before Lieutenant Washington crash-landed his jet. There can be no way he was involved in the death." Dammit, this was so puzzling. Why had the man tried to kill her? What did Washington and Saunders have in common that they were both targeted? Sia was convinced they both had been. The manner of their "accidents" was too similar and the same exact issue with the radar couldn't have been a coincidence. The Navy was meticulous in maintaining their aircraft. Safety was about protecting their investment in the pilots who flew the sleek fighter jets and the amount of money that was tied up in each piece of high-tech machinery.

"There would be if he tampered with the plane before he died."

She hadn't considered that. But what was irking her was the incoherency of the pilot. "That's a possibility, but why didn't Lieutenant Washington correct the position of his plane before he landed? Any seasoned pilot would have. Lieutenant Washington has executed dozens of carrier landings. His behavior doesn't jive with his training and skill. If a drug was administered, then the master chief would have had to be present in the wardroom before Saunders took off."

Chris considered her words, pressing his back to the bulkhead. "There is information we don't have right now, like the autopsy and the condition of his plane. We'll wait for those before we start building conspiracy theories."

"Well, at the very least, the tie I was hoping existed between my brother's death and Lieutenant Saunders's accident could still be viable, but I'm not sure what it means that we have another similar accident within only a day of Lieutenant Saunders's."

Chris straightened. "You suspect Walker had something to do with sabotaging my fighter?"

"I think he had some beef against pilots. Who knows? Maybe he was a wannabe. But I believe he sabotaged your jet."

"Why do you think that?"

"He told me so."

Chris leaned on the small table, his eyes intent and a bit angry. "He told you? He said he sabotaged my plane? He is directly responsible for Rafe's death? Why didn't you tell me this information before?"

She shook her head, holding up her hand. "Wait. No, he didn't exactly tell me that. He just hinted at the information he had no intention of sharing with me that your pilot error was the same as Lieutenant Saunders's. That he somehow had something to do with it. The rest is my conjecture."

"He could have been baiting you. We can't jump to conclusions."

Sia knew he was in charge and the yoke of that rankled. But she wasn't going to shut up just because he thought her ideas were speculation. It was a way for her to work out her cases. Too bad if he didn't like it. "It's possible he could have tampered with your plane," she insisted, getting satisfaction at the way his eyes snapped.

"It is possible. He was on the *McCloud* when Rafe

and I were stationed here. But we have a lot more investigating to do before we come up with an answer."

"I know that. I'm convinced it's worth trying to get them to reopen the case."

"It's a tall order, Sia. The Navy isn't going to be thrilled to rehash an incident that's already been ruled as pilot error. The report states I'm guilty of channelized attention and it substantially contributed to the mishap."

There was a limit to her patience. Sia was well aware of Chris's ruling. His attention had been so consumed with the radar problem it kept him from recognizing and correcting the airspeed and flight path errors and led to his crashing into her brother's plane. Chris was able to eject to safety, but her brother had been unable to do so in time. They had found him in his plane, still strapped in the seat.

"They will if I have new evidence or a confession from the killer," she snapped.

He noted her anger with a mocking glance, skepticism in his eyes. "That's true, but you have to be prepared to accept the fact they made the correct ruling. I was examined by a doctor and he found nothing wrong with me physically. Both Rafe and I were guilty of pilot error. It cost Rafe his life. It cost me…everything."

A wave of exhaustion hit her. She wanted him to see the possibility, but he was trapped in what the Navy had told him. Sia just wasn't convinced. Her voice rose a fraction. "Nevertheless, even if there is a small possibility, I won't rest until justice is served."

Chris scrutinized her pose, her expression, the passion in her voice, and smiled wryly. "You were born to be a prosecutor, Sia." His gaze intensified, sharpened, as if he had sensed something in her. Slowly he closed the gap between them until he was a little too close.

"You'll help me get the evidence I need, won't you, Chris?" Even though it was a question, Sia had no intention of accepting anything but his acquiescence.

Chris shrugged, avoiding the penetrating stare she turned on him. "What does it matter, Sia? I'm no longer part of the Navy and I'll never fly a fighter jet again." His voice was low and smoky like his eyes, laced with old bitterness.

She crossed her arms and scowled at him. "I care. I want my brother's name cleared."

"Your voice is like a loaded gun, Sia." Chris's gaze melted over her, lingering on her mouth. She just realized he had boxed her in.

"Take it any way you want," she said flatly, and pointedly extricated herself from the tight space he'd cornered her into. "But I would think you would jump at the chance." She was all crisp business and haughty demeanor now. It helped to hide the hurt and disappointment that shouldn't be as crushing as they were. "My brother didn't have a chance to defend himself. He didn't have a voice in the matter. I will be that voice for him." She moved back into the main part of the cabin with a deliberate calm that cost her more than he'd ever realize.

"I'll do what I can."

Sia's jaw tightened fractionally. There was still the thread of disappointment he hadn't been more supportive of her plan. He hadn't been there when the master chief had told her he knew something but wasn't telling her anything. That he expected her to go to her grave knowing the two men she loved most in the world hadn't been responsible for the accident. She wanted to grab his shoulders and shake him and make him question every aspect, every memory of that day. But he seemed resigned to his fate and hadn't even considered something else could have been at fault. And, as irrational as it might be, that hurt. "That's all I can ask," she said grudgingly.

"I think we should focus our attention fully on the case we're investigating right now, Sia. Saunders and Washington deserve that."

Sia nodded. "They do."

"Do we have Saunders's autopsy yet?"

Sia shifted her eyes away from his and hedged. She hadn't meant to lie to him, but unless he directly asked Billy about when she received the report, he would never know she had it in her briefcase. She was just being contrary and she knew it. Being under his thumb for her every move on this case rankled. "I'm not sure. Once the case closed and I was sent home, I really didn't have a chance to follow up." All true.

"Well, that needs to be one of our priorities. NCIS agents always follow up."

She nodded. "Agreed. I could look into that right now. I've just got to find Billy."

"Sia, he's probably turned in. It's late."

"It is?"

"Yes, and you're dead on your feet. Let's put this on hold until tomorrow when we'll both be rested. We need to organize how we're going to tackle and untangle this mess. If Walker is responsible for all three deaths, then we need to figure that out. If not, we need to either confirm the pilot-error ruling or negate it. There's more at stake here than proving innocence or guilt."

"What is that?"

"There are families involved. People who want to know what happened to their loved ones. They need to have answers to put them completely to rest," he said gently.

He opened the cabin door and Sia stepped out. He followed and secured the door. He turned and headed down the corridor and she followed.

It must have been the weariness leeching at her body. His words caused a storm of emotions to rise in her, the remembered pain of her brother's death and shame that it had been deemed his fault, never knowing the real answers, not being able to forgive or forget Chris's part in his death. The tantalizing clue from Walker that he had the real answer, but had no intention of giving her that peace. Her eyes filled and she stumbled on the ladder, which was just what the Navy called the metal stairway that led to the various decks of the ship.

With lightning-quick reflexes, Chris caught her and the movement jostled her sore shoulder. She cried out at the painful twinge. Chris responded by steadying her and swinging her up into his arms. Against her protests, he carried her the rest of the way to her quarters.

The memories whirled around her and intertwined, mixing in a braid of pain and longing that had pulled at her for six long years. To feel his touch again was torture. To have his arms around her again confused her, but was still wonderful.

He was sorely testing her sense of balance. Seeing him again was both unexpected and unwanted. At least

on her end. She was going to have to endure working
with him—she didn't have a real choice, but she could
ill afford to let herself rekindle any of the feelings she'd
had for him. She couldn't risk it. Besides, their forced
contact was temporary, so there was no point. All she
had to do was resist the temptation—the very potent
temptation.

"Put me down," she demanded for the third time. Defiantly, he held her against his warm, muscular body.
"It was unnecessary."

"You're dead on your feet and this was faster."

His voice had gone rough like whiskey and smoke
with a touch of black satin sheets. Sia's body responded
swiftly and automatically to those softly uttered words,
nonsensical as they were. He might have said anything
in that voice, and she feared her response would have
been the same—an instantaneous quickening, a flash
of warmth, reduced lung capacity. His breath was warm
against her cheek. "I don't need you to rescue me." She
clenched her teeth at the breathless quality to her voice.

"You were always fiercely independent." A wicked
gleam sparkled in his eyes, curling the corners of his
delectable mouth. He leaned close as he easily held her
in his strong arms, his thumb rubbing against the exposed skin between her sleeve and the sling. The feel of
his skin against her sent a shower of sparks through her.

"Damn straight," she said as his gaze intensified and
there was more fire in his eyes than smoke. With little
effort, he caught her gaze, held her prisoner.

"And stubborn," he breathed, leaning closer still, his
lips just brushing the shell of her ear.

She gave him a look that made better men back off

and ground her teeth when he only smiled at her. She wiggled against him and he sighed deep in his chest. Finally, he let her go with a slow slide down his body. For far too long, he kept one arm wrapped around her, as if he couldn't quite bear to let her go.

He had often accused her of being obstinate, and those words brought a rush of bittersweet emotion so strong Sia had to take a moment to compose herself. She was finding it almost as difficult to move out of his embrace.

"My independence has served me well," she said.

"I have no doubt."

He fell silent again, and maybe it was her own mounting tension over the swelling emotional war she was playing with herself that made the air between them seem to crackle. But, at least from her perspective, the awareness and anxiety were operating on another level, as well.

He turned as if to go and she risked a quick sideways glance at him then; she couldn't help it. His profile was solemn, his jaw hard and set. His gaze was fixed on a point at the end of the passageway. This emotion she felt could be totally one-sided. Chances were, he didn't want or desire anything from her other than her collaboration on this case.

She was thankful no one had witnessed her momentary breakdown. She leaned against the door frame and tried to tell herself all the reasons why being disappointed with that probable reality was a really dangerous way to feel.

"Sia, there's no shame in accepting help."

It was a struggle to find her composure. He was far

too close, and every facet of her equilibrium was threat-ened, physically, emotionally, intellectually. "There is when I'm an officer in the Navy and in an official ca-pacity aboard an aircraft carrier. I didn't need to defend my professionalism before you showed up at JAG and hijacked my case."

"I didn't hijack your case."

"Yes, you did. When you hijacked it, you wouldn't back down or reassign someone else. You refused. Now we have this…"

She trailed off.

"This?"

"Never mind. I'm going to bed." She turned her back to him and grabbed the handle to open the stateroom door. She felt shame at the need to escape.

"No, wait a minute. You can't leave it hanging like that."

"Chris, I don't want to rehash old news or old feel-ings. It's been too long and we both know what we had ended when my brother died. That's the end of the story."

There was that palpable danger again. His hand slipped over hers on the doorknob. She could feel how close he was to her, her back tingling with his nearness, the heat of him. The situation between them was spiral-ing out of control. All the more reason to get the inves-tigation back on track. She'd think everything through later, figure out what to do about it. When he was far, far away and not looking at her the way he had looked at her. Like he still wanted to consume her.

And, damn her memories, she knew what it would be like to let him.

"Is it? I think you still feel something, Sia."

"No." But her protest was low and breathless.

And if Chris himself wasn't dangerous, then what she felt when he was this near surely was. She couldn't fall for him, not for his body or his tarnished soul or his allure of the forbidden. There was no room in her life for this man. She couldn't have her heart broken again; she was still trying to glue the pieces back together from the last time she had come apart.

But she couldn't seem to remove her hand. It seemed a lifeline, an anchor that bolstered her as the memories, good and bad, flashed over her like an uncontrollable fire.

He grasped her hand and turned her toward him and she was powerless to resist.

Holding her breath, she counted the beats of her heart, her eyes on his, wondering why she didn't take her own advice and let go. Walk away.

His hand squeezed hers and his eyes softened. "Sia," he said, his voice low and textured like raw silk—rough and smooth at once, beckoning a woman to reach out and touch him, tempting her, luring her closer.

Her eyes met his and she was lost in the dark gray depths, so lost. It was as if the world and their problems melted in the heat of their eyes. She trembled with the longing she had buried for six years while she immersed herself in her work to forget. She didn't know if it was her near-death experience, the medication, or her deep-seated longing for him. She swayed forward, into him.

His arms slipped around her, taking her mouth without preamble, his lips sizzling against hers. For the first time in Sia's life, she found herself losing control when she very much needed to maintain control, needed to keep her distance. But she lost her train of thought as her good arm slipped up around his neck, her fingers tangling through his hair. He opened his mouth wider, taking more of her. She knew a single kiss wasn't going to be enough.

His mouth was made for love, for kissing and making love, so soft and lush and captivating. She moved against him, her breasts pressing against his chest, her mouth angling over his and creating a brief moment of suction, and as quickly as that, heat shot through every single inch of her body. She felt her control slip, a quick jerk of it out from under her.

Sia was drowning. Drowning in desire and confusion—and desire won, every second, every heartbeat. She wasn't proud of it. She should be made of sterner stuff.

She had to stop. But she couldn't remember why. It was more than a kiss, more than any kiss he'd ever given her. And her mind focused on that one thought—shamelessly. The feel of him in her mouth, the taste of him, was intoxicating, compulsive. He set her on fire with his kiss, made her gasp, and every inch of her wanted more. It was wild. Wild and hot and utterly sexual in a way she'd thought she would never know except in her fantasies—but the reality of it, damn, the reality of it was so much more intense. The silkiness of his hair sliding through her fingers, the rough edge of his jaw beneath her palm, the strength of his arms wrapped around her. Fantasies were perfect because they were so safe. She was in control. Chris epitomized the loss of control. There was no safety in those dark eyes. The pure physical energy of him was a force to be reckoned with. He was powerful, dangerous and unpredictably seductive.

And she'd be a fool if she thought they could ever have what they'd lost. With a soft cry she pulled away.

"I can't!" Her eyes filled. She hadn't meant to cry, but her barriers were frayed and she was so tired.

"Why?"

Tears spilled out and ran down her cheeks. "You know why." She reached for anything that would put distance between them. "Because of your error the Navy memorial has refused to honor my brother. He was a hero and he's never going to get the recognition he deserved."

Chris stood there, taking her words like physical blows. His dark eyes were haunted and filled with the guilt she knew he felt and she regretted her words. Bashing him wouldn't change anything. Rafael was dead. Her parents were dead. Everyone she loved had been taken from her. If she could find any connection, anything at all to the fact it might have been murder, then she could exonerate her brother. And, in turn, Chris.

Standing there stoically and taking what she had to say right on the chin only made her realize how strong and brave he was. He didn't flinch or get angry, he just stood there and let her vent. She didn't know what to say. She could only feel, feel her heart break, feel her mind try to find a way to reconcile her emotions.

But she couldn't move that immovable wall. She couldn't seem to step forward, past it. It remained, lingering, holding her hostage. Nowhere to go.

Nowhere to run.

He reached out gently and wiped at the tears on her cheek with his thumb, then abruptly he pulled her hard against him. His hand disrupted her bun and sent her hair cascading down her back. He buried his face in her shoulder. "Do me a favor, Sia?"

Her voice, clogged with emotion, was muffled against his shoulder. "What?"

"Keep an open mind?"

She took a deep breath. "Keep an open mind?"

"Yes. Can you do that?" he asked, his voice a shade rougher.

"I'll try," she responded, her voice breaking. "I'll try."

He released her and walked away, his broad back disappearing down the passageway. For one moment, she let herself dream they had a chance, but she knew it was a lie. If he hadn't been so stubborn and had just assigned someone else to this case, it would have been so much easier for both of them. Anger mixed in with the desire and longing.

Slipping into her quarters, she burst into tears, her throat tight, her chest heavy. In the darkness, she let herself cry for the loss, for the memories and for the love she once had for a man who could no longer comfort her.

Chapter 5

He hadn't meant to watch her. He'd only come up to the flight deck to run off some of his disappointment and the desire that had caught him off guard last night, and Sia was already there. Of course, that kiss shouldn't have had him tossing and turning, but it had.

He'd been craving the taste of her since last night. He'd convinced himself he must have exaggerated the hell out of what it had been like to kiss her, because a kiss was just a kiss, right? No way could one kiss be so special, so addicting, so enthralling…so intense.

As it turned out, he had forgotten the impact. *In a big way.*

Her lips had been so soft, and the way her breath hitched in the back of her throat, accompanied by that small, rough moan, immediately made him go rock-hard. It was all he could do not to plaster her back against the bulkhead and take and give until they were both sated.

She'd taken off the sling and was easily moving across the flight deck as if she hadn't been almost murdered two days ago. Her dark, curly hair was caught up in a ponytail, streaming out behind her like ebony ribbons as her legs, encased in black Lycra, fueled her quick strides.

The bruise still stood starkly out on her soft, deep-golden skin, but it was beginning to fade somewhat.

"You going to run, sir, or lollygag?" a flight deck sailor said good-naturedly as he walked past. "Although it's a very nice view." He smiled and returned back inside the carrier, no doubt on some task that needed completing. The work on a ship as large as this one never ceased.

Chris stretched and took off. It wasn't long before he caught up with her. "Are you sure you should be running? You almost got up close and personal with the ocean just a few days ago."

"Yeah, swimming with the fishes isn't my idea of fun." She turned to look at him, not at all shy about what had happened last night. He remembered that was something he had always liked about Sia. Her straightforward manner and her lack of game playing had attracted him from the moment he'd met her. Her acerbic wit and quick comebacks made him admire her even more. It was as if six years had melted away.

They were quiet for a few paces and then Sia spoke. "I have a couple of things I need to confess."

She glanced over at him, but there was no apology in her eyes. Instead he saw a flash of anger. He suspected she had no intention of sharing with him what she was up to, but somehow had changed her mind. He wondered why.

"Well, get the torpedoes in the water then."

She laughed without mirth. "Nothing as explosive or dangerous as that. But I want you to know."

"So it doesn't come back to bite you on the butt?"

"Something like that. Even though you hijacked my case, I guess I can be magnanimous in sharing with you some of my suspicions. After all, we're really on the same mission."

"We are. We just have a lot of baggage to jettison."

She chose not to respond to the personal tensions between them. He could feel it even now as they started another lap on the deck. He was sweating freely now, but his body was warming up to the exercise, his muscles loosening.

"After my run-in with Walker and his intriguing statements, I told my legalman to do some research on the deaths aboard the *McCloud* and other ships in the fleet to see if there are any correlations. It might give us a baseline and data to see if we have a consistent MO. It will also tell us if Walker was in the vicinity of any other *accidents*."

"And the second confession?"

"I stalled you on the autopsy for Saunders."

Chris stopped in midstride, floored. After a few steps forward, Sia jogged back. She took his hand and propelled him forward. "Don't stop running. We haven't finished enough to cool down yet."

"I'm not about to cool down anytime soon," he

growled, anger beating in rhythm with his blood. "Why?"

She didn't flinch under his steady, snapping gaze.

"I didn't have a chance to look it over," she said with a bit of miff in her tone. "I wanted to do so without you looking over my shoulder. I have a copy in my briefcase in my quarters. Billy gave it to me as soon as I met up with him yesterday in the legal office. I read through it after you dropped me off at my stateroom last night."

She offered him no apology and he could understand why. Sia considered this her case and he was along for the ride. Regardless of what her commanding officer said, Sia wasn't one to relinquish what she considered her responsibility. He understood this woman all too well. Okay, so she had more at stake than he did. She wanted to clear her brother's name, get him memorialized and bring a killer to justice on a case she thought she may have botched. Chris was sure she thought she could nail all those tasks. When Sia was on a mission, everyone needed to watch out. He just hoped she wasn't setting herself up for disappointment.

There was something else niggling at him and he didn't want to fully acknowledge it lest he also set himself up for disappointment, but he couldn't help it. She had him to gain.

What if she wanted him back? What if she could justify to herself the accident had been foul play? Would she then be able to forgive him? Would that be enough for him? He wasn't sure.

And that eye-opener changed his entire outlook of his world to some new focus, as if he was looking through a kaleidoscope, trying to make sense of the chaotic colors with a view that was no longer his own to interpret—a potentially danger-filled view. It should have scared him more. He was feeling suddenly off-kilter, like the slowly pitching ship.

Sia's speed diminished and finally slowed to a walk. She was giving him sidelong glances as if he would suddenly explode. He was partly angry and partly frustrated she hadn't trusted him with this information. They walked in silence to the exit that would lead them from the flight deck back down into the belly of the ship.

They reached the point where they had to part ways and, without preamble, Chris grabbed Sia's good elbow and steered her into a shadowed alcove. "You have a lot of nerve."

"Me?" Her chin angled with challenge and her voice was brittle. "You wouldn't take the easy way out. You never do, Chris."

"I'm in command here, Sia. You will not withhold information from me again. Is that clear?"

She breathed a heated sigh and faced him defiantly. "Not now, Chris. Not here."

"Yes, now. Yes, here. Not everything is on your terms!"

And just like that she exploded. "I answer to the Navy, not to NCIS, Chris."

He didn't miss the fact he'd said almost those same words to her. Throwing them in his face only made his ire grow. "I was there when your commanding officer gave you a direct order, so for all intents and purposes you do answer to NCIS. You answer to me."

"What?" she scoffed.

"This isn't a joke, Sia." She shoved at him, but he didn't let her push him away.

He knew she was tired, the kind of tired you didn't get from one difficult day. But he had to be tough with Sia or he would lose ground with her. She was much too strong a personality to back down when she thought she was right. But he wasn't perfect. He lost his grip a little, too. "You could severely damage your JAG career by being insubordinate."

"Is that a threat?" she shouted right back at him. "Are you going to write me up, Chris? For doing my job! Right now I care more about the truth then I care about my JAG career."

"That's evident," he shot back. "But you will heed my authority."

"I chafe at your authority. NCIS is a civilian agency. You don't have anything but a fine thread of influence. This should have been my case. It all started with me and me alone. That's where it should end."

"I was there when it started. Don't forget that," he said flatly.

"How can I forget that? How can I? It destroyed my life." Her words were precise, old fury barely reined in. "Not a day goes by I don't think about it and how it eviscerated me."

He flinched and took a step back at the anguish in her voice. The pain was as sharp as ever, as sharp as a razor blade that had ended his dream of a Navy career, lost him the love of his life, deprived him of the best friend who'd been so like a brother to him, destroyed his hope for a family. It sliced at his heart, mocked him with its cruelty, tried to sever his strength.

Regret burned like acid in his throat, behind his eyes. He clenched his jaw against it, whipped himself mentally to get past it. But it all came rushing back, breaking out of its six-year-old prison. And with it came the sound of his father's voice. His father had been a mean, drunken, good-for-nothing bastard who had told him time and again he would never make anything out of himself. Never be anything. But he'd been smart, smarter than he'd let on, because his father would have taken away every opportunity he had to excel. He would make sure his father never saw his grades. Not that his father ever cared. As soon as he could, he applied to and got accepted into the Naval Academy in Annapolis with his eye on Top Gun and becoming a fighter pilot. The tests were a piece of cake, and the training fit him like a well-worn glove. He had owned the skies for a brief time, as fleeting as the burst of fireworks as they lit up the night sky. It wasn't long before he plunged to earth.

"Oh, God, Chris. I'm sorry. I didn't mean to say that." She brought a hand to her mouth to hold back the cry that tore through her, but the tears still flooded and fell. He struggled with the burden of his guilt. He braced his shoulders against it, trembling inside.

"Chris," she said softly. "I lost so much and it's built up for so long. I never got the chance to tell you how angry I was with you. How devastated."

He closed his eyes, the pain and longing had haunted him for so long, closer to the surface than they had ever been. She touched his shoulder, gripping him as if he were her lifeline, but he knew better.

"You have a right to your feelings, Sia." But God, it

hurt, because she might not have meant to say it, but she was most definitely feeling it.

Then she cupped his face. He opened his eyes and the glistening of her tears totally did him in. He wished he could go back to that day and perish with Rafe. It would have been so much easier to have just simply died.

Her eyes softened as she stared up into his face, remorse as clear as the fine brandy color of her eyes. He wanted far, far more than either of them could give at the moment.

He ran his thumb along her lower lip, watching her eyes darken under his touch, wishing like hell her dragons had already been slain.

But he knew he was one of those dragons.

"We have to keep everything in perspective. We just agreed up on the deck we were in this together." His voice sounded raw and misused.

Sia dropped her gaze and took a moment to gather herself. Breathing deeply, she wiped at her eyes. "I'm always so damn angry. It serves me well in court, but it's murder on relationships." She tried to laugh, but it was half-hearted.

"We owe it to those pilots, Sia. If they were victims, we need to bring out the truth and put a stop to the murders."

She nodded. "We're in total agreement about that."

"About our past, we should bury it and try not to let it interfere with our investigation. I understand how you feel, but you have to abide by the orders you were given."

Temper flared in her eyes, but she banked it. "I'll participate in the investigation." She didn't give an inch and he accepted that. They would probably clash again, but for now the storm was over.

Then without warning her arms went around his neck and she hugged him hard. He stroked her hair and kissed her temple and some of the pain she'd inflicted leeched away.

Sia was so torn, so confused. Their private and professional lives were at odds, but her emotions—damn, they were making her crazy.

Dumping on him had been so wrong, but it released a lot of pressure inside her. It was all so much—unburdening herself, trying to reconcile her feelings for him and her anger toward him, then this…overload of sensations with him holding her, caring about her.

He tipped her head back so their gazes could meet. She trembled a little, wanted to be strong enough to scoot away, but had the presence of mind to finally admit to herself this felt good. It was time they hashed out their past. It was time it was dealt with and then she could walk away and have it resolved.

They held each other for several minutes. Like a fog settling over her, the gray of his eyes held her steadfastly and all she could think was she wanted to be able to look into his whenever she wanted to. Like this, intimate and personal, or across a crowded room, when nothing more than a quick smile would say everything that needed to be said between them. She had lost that and that loss left a deeper hole than anything else.

She started to speak, to try to find the words, but he tucked her against his chest then, and she knew there'd come a time when she would say what was on her mind, no matter how painful. Reality had a way of intruding to keep her locked up in a situation that seemed to have no end. But she was on the scent now and she wouldn't let up until the truth was revealed. She had to have that. Lieutenants Washington and Saunders deserved that. And her sweet, strong, funny brother deserved that.

It was a just cause.

When he finally shifted away from her, she only felt it was too soon.

He kissed her temple, then her cheek.

His expression wasn't readable and that gave her pause. "Go and get cleaned up," he said.

"Is that an order?" she asked, a smile playing with the corners of her mouth.

He shook his head and his lips curved a little, too. "Meet me in the officers' mess when you're ready."

"Should I salute you before I go?"

In response, he lifted her hand up to his lips, kissing the back first, then the palm, before curling her fingers in to seal it there. It was a simple gesture, both intimate and heartbreaking, and because she wanted to hold on tightly to both of those things, knowing what lay ahead, she kept her fingers tightly curled as he responded.

"Get going, wiseass."

Back in her stateroom, she took a quick shower and dressed in her uniform, eager to get to the mess and food. She was starving. She was also ready to continue with the investigation. She mentally reminded herself to check her email to see if there had been any news from her legalman.

Stepping outside, she slipped her briefcase strap over her shoulder and turned toward the mess.

Sia was jostled by several crewmembers as she made

her way to the mess. A lot of hungry sailors were crowding the companionway and the ladders. Sia got her bearings and turned toward the ladder. The way cleared a bit and Sia started down. Suddenly, she felt hands on her back and someone gave her a shove.

Losing her balance, Sia began to fall. Only the quick reflexes of the sailor in front of her kept her and him from falling the rest of the way. She apologized and he smiled and told her it was no problem. Once she righted herself, she glanced over her shoulder, but all she saw was the glimpse of dark clothing disappearing down the companionway, getting lost in the sea of sailors.

Had someone just pushed her? It had felt as if the hands had applied force. Maybe it had been an accident and the sailor was afraid Sia would reprimand him or her. She shrugged it off and reached the deck where the mess was located.

She saw Chris near the door to the mess and she stopped on the stairs. She'd forgotten how handsome he was. Age had only tempered those looks, taking him from overtly brash to silently lethal.

He was sorely testing her sense of balance. Their bond, it seemed, was still strong, unexpected as it was unwanted. At least on her end. She found him to be annoyingly irresistible, but she had to be careful not to feel those old feelings and get confused. She could so easily let herself become more attracted to him.

She remembered how he had held her when they'd had that terrible fight after the run on the flight deck. He'd been so solid as he cradled her against his strong chest. It calmed her, soothed her pain in a way that was completely unexpected. He had helped her so much in that moment it caught her off guard and made her realize the strength of their connection.

At that moment, someone he must have known when he'd served aboard the *McCloud* greeted him with a hearty handshake. Chris smiled. It did something magical to his face, disarming her and making her sigh. What would it take for him to smile like that at her? Too many memories flooded her and her regret was never more poignant than it was at this moment. The man moved on but the smile in Chris's eyes lingered.

When he turned and saw her, it diminished some, but didn't completely fade. With a small smile of her own, she made her way over to where he stood.

They went inside, got their food and sat down. She opened up her briefcase and handed him Lieutenant Saunders's autopsy report. "I won't say anything until you finish reading it."

He nodded and as he ate his eggs, his eyes fastened to the pages. Sia still resented her commanding officer's orders. She didn't want her hands tied in handling this investigation. But she had been right when she'd told Chris he didn't have that much of a hold over her.

So what if she was reprimanded. She was going to do what it took to finish this once and for all.

Chris looked up from the pages, his eyes a strong, steady gray, unique and compelling. "They found nothing in his tox screen."

"Right, but look at this." She pulled out the report from the flight boss and handed it to him. Forking up some fluffy eggs, Sia said, "The lieutenant was complaining of dizziness and then he went incoherent." Sliding the fork in her mouth, she chewed and swallowed.

Chris accepted the report and looked at the testimony. "That could have been hypoxemia, caused by a bad oxygen mix."

Sia nodded. "It could have, but then there would have been evidence of that on the report—his lungs or brain or even the oxygenation of his blood would have revealed that." She tapped the autopsy report. "The ME cited nothing in the report that would have indicated he was oxygen-starved." She flipped to the final part of the autopsy. "In fact, Lieutenant Saunders's cause of death is drowning. But if he was impaired during the flight and it didn't have anything to do with hypoxemia, then it had to have been something else."

Hard and sharp, his gaze cut to her. "Like what?"

She met his eyes and shrugged. "Well, an allergy to something he hadn't been exposed to before is possible." She paused for a moment and said, "But it could also be caused by ingesting a drug."

He reached out and snagged his coffee cup and took a sip. "What drug?"

She leaned back in her chair in frustration. "I don't know. I confiscated an over-the-counter irregularity product from the master chief's locker, but the bottle was lost after he took it from me." She could still see his smug smile and she was convinced the man had been harboring more than the secret of what was in the bottle. It was possible he could have been killing pilots. Or know the person responsible, if there was such a person.

"So what makes you suspicious that Saunders was drugged?"

Pushing away the emotion that was distracting her, she reached for logic. "That's the kicker. The master chief himself. When he talked about the accidents, he shook the bottle. I got permission to search his rack after Saunders's wingman swore an oath he saw the master chief touch Saunders's coffee cup. So he had the opportunity to put whatever was in that bottle into Saunders's coffee cup."

Chris closed the autopsy report and handed it back to her for safekeeping. "Still, all the evidence we have is circumstantial at this point, along with some healthy speculation."

Sia nodded. "Playing devil's advocate?"

He shrugged. "You did enough mock trials in law school to know about that. There's always somebody who can trip you up if you're not prepared."

She nodded, remembering those lessons from the simulated jury trials she'd participated in as a law student. "I know it's circumstantial, but my gut tells me there was or is a liar and a killer on this ship. Lieutenants Saunders and Washington were only the latest victims. I think that you or my brother somehow got caught in that same killer's sights."

"A conspiracy? Is that what you're thinking?"

"I don't know." She tucked the report back into her briefcase. "Yet. But I'll find out."

"We will find out, together."

The inflection on the word *together* held a deeper, more intimate meaning. There was a time she welcomed that meaning, but now all she wanted to do was put distance between them. It kept her focused and sane.

She shivered a little, thinking about how he'd tasted, how he'd kissed as if no time had passed whatsoever, as if they knew each other in a more profound way than even on a physical level. No, she firmly decided. No more of those thoughts. A couple of kisses was already two too many. But she found her eyes falling to his mouth. He didn't miss the movement and his gray eyes went steamy.

She decided the best bet was to ignore it completely. "I couldn't go to court with this kind of evidence. But Chris, even if he had a bottle that was run-of-the-mill medication, it doesn't mean that's what was actually in the bottle."

He smiled, but it didn't diminish one whit the heat in his gaze. "That is true. I don't take anything at face value."

She mused for a moment, a thought coalescing in her brain. "All this negative evidence does add up to something."

"You have a theory." He rose and gathered up his dirty dishes and she did the same. "It's not a bad thing to talk out alternatives. You never know what correlation we might draw, or be able to put together some other lead we might have missed. Speculation isn't a bad thing, even if it's wrong. So let's hear it."

Dumping her trash and placing her dishes in the proper place, Sia turned to him. She wanted to be mad at him, even though she realized it was just an excuse to focus her feelings of helplessness on something tangible. Or someone. Instead, she took a deep breath and let it out slowly, forcing herself to relax. Getting worked up wasn't going to help matters any. Besides, she'd already gotten worked up enough for one day. Her gaze slid sideways across the busy mess as Chris's hand cupped her elbow to steer her through the crowd. It was more of a mechanism to keep them together so he could hear what she was saying. The warmth of his hand shouldn't affect her so, but it was like a jolt of electricity. She reined in her thoughts. "In lieu of any evidence the pilot was impaired or his system was faulty, the Navy will rule it pilot error and close the books."

Chris's lips thinned and his voice rasped out. "And a killer goes free."

Her eyes solemn, Sia nodded. "And a killer goes free."

Chapter 6

Chris followed Sia up the ladder, unable to keep his eyes from her shapely backside. He remembered what it was like to cup her there, to hold her hips against his, giving him the leverage he needed to thrust deep inside her. His gaze traveled up the surprisingly unwrinkled and fresh uniform to her shoulders, remembering how creamy they were, how soft her skin was, so smooth and warm. When Sia looked back down pensively, he hesitated and turned around to look behind him. "You all right?" he asked, meeting her eyes.

She dropped her gaze, and said, "Yes, I almost fell here on the way to meet you at the mess."

"Lost your footing?" he said, his gaze steady on her.

"I must have," she said with a shrug.

He stepped closer to her and he noticed how her body tightened. "You don't sound certain."

"I'm not. It seemed as if I'd been pushed. But I didn't

see anyone and there were a number of people coming down the ladder."

After the talk about a possible killer aboard the carrier, Chris wasn't about to take any chances. "How about you stick with me next time we head for food?"

Sia smiled and his heart stumbled a little. Okay, a lot.

"Ready to hold my hand again," she said with a teasing tone.

It was so much like the old Sia, Chris felt a familiar tug of longing that was almost painful. He smiled back at her and said softly, "I'll always be there for you, sweetheart."

Her smile faded. "That sounded a bit sarcastic. Are you implying something?"

"Just letting you know I have your back." Maybe he had said it that way. Maybe his resentment at her ability to turn her back on him was finally starting to show. Maybe it was time for her to know what she had done to him.

Their gazes met, warred. If the barb stung, she made sure not to show it. He could almost see her defenses surge, click into place. "But I didn't have yours. That's what you're saying, isn't it?"

He brought his mouth within a whisper of her lips, the potent connection between them made volatile by the words he refused to say. Some people had to come to their own conclusions. "Guilt is a strange emotion, Sia. It comes out of nowhere to hammer at you. It sometimes hides in the shadows, but it dictates every single thing you do. It's a relentless master."

"Guilt? What do I have to feel guilty about?"

Pointing anything out to a person who was unaware

of why they felt the way they did was not productive. Sick of that kernel of pain inside his gut that abraded him relentlessly, he said, "You decide what I'm saying, since you seem to like to put words in my mouth."

"Oh, forget it. We don't have time for this."

The sheen of pain in her eyes gave her away, but he let her retreat. He knew what it was like when guilt cut deep. There would be a better time and place. "Right, Sia. It's all dead and buried in the past." He brushed past her. "Let's get back to the legal office and line up our interviews for today."

"Who's on your primary list?" she said, catching up to him.

"Anyone who touched that plane or had any interaction with the pilot."

She stopped and turned to look at him. "That's going to be a long list."

"Then we'd better get started."

Back at the office, she settled into a chair behind the small table she had previously used for interviews.

She pulled her laptop out of her briefcase and set it on the table. "I think it would be best to organize this by area. That way we're not wasting our time by backtracking."

"Agreed."

"We've already interviewed the airman who had direct communication with Lieutenant Washington. So I'd like to talk to everyone who was on duty that day."

"We could systematically move down from Pri-Fly to the Flight Deck Control and Launch Operation Room," Chris said.

Sia responded, "That's where the handling officer and his crew play with their paper planes?"

Chris snorted. "Right, the table is called the *Ouija Board,* a two-level transparent plastic table with etched outlines of the flight deck and hangar deck. Each aircraft is represented by a scale aircraft cutout on the table. The handlers use those cutouts to represent real planes as they move on and off the carrier. When one is in maintenance, they turn it over."

"So anyone who works in that room knows when a specific plane is down for maintenance?" Sia asked.

"That's correct. Handy for a killer to keep track of both Saunders's and Washington's planes."

"Yes, handy indeed," Sia said.

Sia pulled up the list and jotted down a few names according to priority. "What's next?" she asked. "The control centers, including the Carrier Air Traffic Control Center and the Combat Direction Center?"

Chris nodded. "We will want to speak to the landing signal officer and crew that were present when the jet crashed, along with getting the footage of the crash, as well. The captain can get us that information."

"I think we have enough for now. Let's get started." They made their way out of the legal office and were soon ascending the ladder to Pri-Fly. The skipper wasn't present at this time. Instead, the OOD, or officer of the deck, took his place to stand a four-hour watch. Chris and Sia split up the list and took statements from each of the crew members who had been present during the crash of Lieutenant Washington's fighter.

When they met at the end of the interviews, Chris asked, "Anything pop?"

"No, nothing of significance that I could detect."

"Okay, let's move down to the next deck and then question the handling officer, Lieutenant Susan Cotes."

The Flight Deck Control and Launch Operation Room was small—smaller than Chris remembered. He wedged himself inside the windowless room, followed closely by Sia. The close confines intensified the smell of her fresh hair and the subtle smell he would always define as Sia. Trying to minimize his distraction, he turned slightly away from her. Lieutenant Cotes was a tall, quite beautiful woman with dark brown hair and sharp green eyes. She was wearing the yellow tunic that identified her as an air handler.

After introducing themselves, Chris said, "Lieutenant Cotes, we'd like to ask you a few questions regarding the day Lieutenant Washington crash-landed his fighter jet on the *McCloud*."

"Yes, sir. Anything I can do to help."

"All the information you received from the flight deck LSO was accurate that day?"

"Yes, Lieutenant Jackson is always on her game. She tried to wave off Lieutenant Washington, but it was too late. He hit the edge of the carrier and crashed."

"When was the last time Lieutenant Washington's plane was in maintenance?"

Chris noticed how her hand shook as she smoothed it through her hair. He wondered whether it was nerves or something else. "I can't exactly recall, but I can look it up for you and get you the information as soon as possible."

"Did you know Lieutenant Washington?" Sia asked.

"Yes, I did, but only as an acquaintance."

"We'll look forward to receiving that report. Thank you for your time," Chris said.

"She was a little jumpy," Sia said as they made their way to the Combat Direction Center. "Could be the general unrest after a crash or something more."

"Could be."

In the Carrier Air Traffic Control Center, they talked to several radar technicians, including a young man named Ensign Brant, who was new to the position. Once they were done with that, it was long past the lunch hour. They went to get something to eat and then were back in the legal office. When Sia opened her laptop, she let Chris know Lieutenant Cotes had sent her an email giving her a report as to when Lieutenant Washington's plane had last been serviced. "Looks like it was just a week ago, and it looks like the master chief oversaw the repairs. He's the one who signed off on the log."

"That would be significant if the master chief wasn't responsible for just about every plane that went through maintenance."

"True, but it does tie him to Lieutenant Washington. Let's find out who did the actual maintenance."

In the maintenance hangar below the flight deck, Sia and Chris tracked down someone who could give them answers regarding who had actually worked on the plane.

They were directed to a seaman mechanic who was on record as performing the necessary maintenance. "Seaman Yost?"

A young man with dark brown hair and wire-rimmed glasses turned and came immediately to attention. "Officer on the deck," he said.

"At ease, sailor. Are you Yost?"

"That's me. What can I do for you?" Yost relaxed into an at-ease position.

"I'm Special Agent Chris Vargas from NCIS and this is Lieutenant Commander Soto, JAG. We have a few questions for you regarding Lieutenant Eli Washington's jet. We understand you were the one who did the maintenance."

The man straightened when he saw Chris's badge. He looked at Sia and paled a little. "Yes, I did."

"You can continue with your duties," Sia said.

Cleaning a dirty wrench with a red cloth, he set the tool aside and chose another wrench. "Are you saying there was something wrong with the plane and that is why he crashed?" Turning away, he slipped the wrench inside an open panel.

"No. The report hasn't come back yet. Were you the only person who worked on the plane when it was in the bay?" Chris asked.

He stopped what he was doing and faced them. "You're asking me this question because of the master chief." He looked between the two of them.

"Just answer the question, Seaman," Sia said. Her voice brooked no disagreement.

"The master chief was one of the most knowledge-able people I've ever worked for in the Navy. I still have a hard time believing he had anything to do with that other F/18 crash, but the shiner on your face says otherwise."

Sia said nothing.

Seaman Yost sighed. "The master chief went over my work on Lieutenant Washington's fighter."

"Was that unusual?"

"Very. He oversaw all the departments in Maintenance. I was surprised he would take the time to go over my work here in Avionics."

"Were you present at the time?" Sia asked, stepping closer, her voice steely.

"No. I wasn't," Yost said with a tinge of anger in his voice. Chris suspected he didn't like ratting out the master chief, even if he was dead and all evidence pointed to the fact he was guilty. "Ma'am," he added when Sia's eyes narrowed. "He sent me to start work on another jet."

"So it's possible he could have tampered with the plane?" Sia stepped back and eyed the plane Yost was working on.

"Well, that calls for conjecture, ma'am."

Sia stiffened and her head whipped around. "Are you trying to get into trouble, Yost?"

"No, ma'am."

"Then answer the question," she snapped.

"Yes," he ground out. "In my opinion, I'd say he had plenty of time to tamper with the jet."

"What repairs did you perform on the plane?"

For a moment he didn't answer. Then he sighed. "Routine stuff, but I did notice his radar unit was unseated in the brackets and I fixed that."

"As if it was jarred loose?" Chris asked.

"No, as if it was a hurry-up kinda job. I just figured the last mechanic was in a rush to finish the job."

"You didn't report this?"

"Nah, it was something that was minor and I didn't want to bust the guy's chops."

"That's all for now, Seaman Yost."

He nodded and went back to work.

After they were a safe distance away, Chris said, "We've established the master chief had access to Lieutenant Washington's plane. Could it be he killed Washington from beyond the grave?"

"I guess it may have been possible, if he tampered with the plane. We need to light a fire under them to get that plane checked over ASAP."

"I could get my forensics specialist over to where they've taken the plane and we would have a report in twenty-four hours," Chris said.

"He's that good?"

Chris nodded.

"The salvaged plane was taken to a hangar at Hickam Air Force Base. Saunders's jet is there, as well."

Back in the legal office, Chris connected to his forensic specialist.

"Who's the lovely lady?"

"Keep it focused, Math." Math was the resident nerd at NCIS, but he would be what women called cute. Intensely dedicated to his job, Math did notice a nice turn of ankle and a pretty pair of eyes. He had dark hair that was styled in a bowl cut, with bangs on his forehead. He wore a pair of wire-rimmed glasses and had that perpetual look of an eighteen-year-old. He sometimes acted like one. But Chris often let it slide. The kid was brilliant.

"Hi, lovely lady. Swear to God, Vargas, you get all the good assignments."

Sia smiled at the young man on the computer screen.

"Sia, this is Justin Mathis. Don't encourage him." Chris turned back to the screen. "I have a job for you."

"I'm up to my eyeballs, in eyes, so make it fast."

"I'm not going to ask."

"It's best you don't."

"I need you to fly out here and look over a fighter jet for me. I need a report fast."

Math sighed. "Let me guess, twenty-four hours."

"You got it in one."

"Vargas, I can't promise anything until I see the wreck."

"I don't care what anyone else says, Math, you're the best."

"Ha ha. Bye, lovely lady."

"He's very good at his job, so if anyone can get us some answers, Math can."

"I pulled Lieutenant Washington's record and I found something interesting."

"What?"

"Looks like there was a reason Lieutenant Cotes was a bit jumpy."

"Why?"

"She filed a sexual harassment complaint against Lieutenant Washington."

"When?"

"Two weeks ago."

"Nothing against Saunders?"

Sia pulled up the pilot's file. "No, nothing here I see."

"That doesn't mean he wasn't harassing her. Maybe she didn't get a chance to file a complaint."

"It's possible, but from what I heard from his wingman, he didn't seem the type and I didn't find any notes in his rack when I searched."

"We'll search again."

Sia bristled. "Do you think I'm inept? That I can't do a competent search?"

"No, that's not what I was implying. It's possible something got missed. Especially when you're not sure what you're looking for. Now we know what we're looking for."

"In the meantime, let's get Susan Cotes in here for some more questioning."

Chris and Sia were seated when Susan Cotes entered Legal. She was still in her bright yellow tunic as she took a seat at the table across from them.

"I don't know what I can add to what I've already told you," she said, to break the thick tension in the air.

"Oh, I think you do," Sia said. "You neglected to mention you had filed a sexual harassment charge against Lieutenant Washington."

She closed her eyes and took a deep breath. "I wasn't trying to hide it from you," she said quickly. "I didn't want to blurt it out in front of my coworkers."

"Well, we're alone here. Tell us the details now. Did he assault you?"

"No, nothing like that. He was sending me notes. They would be tucked into my uniform or slipped under my door. Once he cornered me in the wardroom and said we should explore the relationship I'd described in a note to him. I had no idea what he was talking about. I wasn't participating in this fantasy note-writing that he was sure was me. I suggested he had me mixed up with someone else. He insisted it was me, and he seemed quite confused by my response. That's when I lodged the complaint. I barely knew him."

"So he'd never initiated direct contact with you before the incident in the wardroom?"

"No. I thought maybe he was shy or something—not that he seemed that way. I'm not about to get involved with a pilot. I'm interested in making the Navy a career. I didn't want to derail it. Lieutenant Washington was a very handsome man, but I just wasn't interested. When I told him so, he seemed completely baffled and said I was a crazy bitch sending him mixed messages."

"Do you have any of these notes?"

"I gave them to the captain when I filed the grievance."

"You submitted your complaint only two days before Washington crashed his plane."

"Yes, it started up about four days before the crash. I didn't want it to get out of hand, so I made the complaint and hoped the captain would reprimand him and it would stop."

"But Washington crashed before the captain had a chance to speak to him?"

"Yes. I'm sorry he's dead. I just wanted him to leave me alone."

"That's all for now, Cotes. We might have more questions for you later."

"Yes, ma'am." She stood and left the cabin.

"How about we split up," Chris suggested. "You go and talk to the captain and I'll question Washington's wingman. He might have some information about Susan Cotes."

Chris shook his head. "I thought we were going to stick together."

"Don't be silly. I just fell. It's nothing to be concerned about. Besides, we need to split up the workload. It's more efficient."

Chris looked skeptical, but nodded. "All right. If you're sure."

Chris headed toward the wardroom and found Lieutenant Monroe drinking coffee at a table. "Hello, Monroe," Chris said, showing the lieutenant his badge. "I wanted to talk to you about Lieutenant Washington's crash."

"Have a seat."

Chris sat down and leaned back in his chair. "What were the conditions like when you both went to land?"

"It was windy, and that's always a tricky landing."

"Thank God for the meatball."

"Amen to that. It got me in safely with no wave-off my first pass, but when Eli went to land, it was a different story. His flying had been somewhat erratic about a half an hour out, but that's understandable as he reported a problem with his radar. So he reported it and we were recalled. Most of the chatter on the radio was about Eli's condition."

"Did he answer?"

"He did, but as the approach got closer, he got more incoherent. Once I landed and taxied off, I no longer was on the radio. I watched as the LSO waved him off, but Eli came in too low and hit the ship. He skidded right past me. I could see him in the cockpit, but he made no attempt to eject. I didn't even realize I was screaming for him to eject. Of course, he couldn't hear me."

"Did he appear to be unconscious to you?"

"He appeared aware, but I only saw him for a split second. If he had ejected, he would have made it."

"Do you know anything about Washington harassing Lieutenant Susan Cotes?"

Monroe sighed. "Eli was shocked when he discovered the woman wasn't interested and it wasn't because of his good looks. Eli never had a problem with the ladies. He said she was into him, but he didn't say why."

"And that's why he was shocked when she filed the sexual harassment charge?"

"Yes, when she told him, he was floored. He called her crazy and accused her of giving him mixed signals."

"He didn't elaborate on what the mixed signals were, though?"

"No. He didn't say. He might have been a ladies man, but he was closemouthed about his exploits."

"A true gentleman, huh?"

"Yeah." Monroe paused. "The scuttlebutt floating around is pilot error. I hope that's not the case. With Saunders's crash and now Eli, there's going to be some serious consequences for us if this is pilot error. A lot of scrutiny."

"Our investigation isn't complete. Let me know if you can think of anything else that might be important."

"Will do."

Sia navigated her way to the captain's quarters and knocked on the door. He answered and she stepped inside. "I have a few questions regarding a sexual harassment charge Lieutenant Susan Cotes filed against Washington."

"You think this is relevant in Washington's death?"

"We still don't have enough evidence he was murdered and we're following the leads we find. Cotes had a beef with Washington."

"She did. She was pretty upset when she came to me about it. It seems shc was confused with the way he was harassing her."

"The notes?"

"Yes."

"Could I see them?"

The captain went to his desk and pulled a file.

Sia opened the file and found the notes were typewritten, with lascivious messages printed on them. They were signed simply "Eli."

"These are not handwritten. If you're wooing a woman, seems like you'd pull out all the stops."

"I'm not sure. I didn't get an opportunity to talk to him before he died."

"Could I have permission to search his rack?"

"Yes, go ahead."

When she turned to leave, the captain's voice stopped her.

"Before you go, Commander, footage of both crashes your partner wanted to review are on this flash drive. I've had some pushback from Senator Washington. He wants answers about his son's death. Unless you want the senator touching down on this carrier, you'd better wrap this up." She reached for the flash drive, but he didn't immediately let go of it. She looked into his piercing blue eyes and realized why he was in command of an aircraft carrier. "He's not alone, Commander. I want them, too."

He let go of the flash drive and Sia tucked it into her briefcase.

"With all due respect, sir, rushing an investigation is counterproductive."

"Noted. Do it right, Commander, and do it fast."

"Yes, sir."

Sia left and headed right to Washington's rack. Donning gloves, she began to search. It wasn't long before she came across folded papers tucked under his mattress. After she opened them and read them, Sia realized they shed a whole new light on Susan Cotes and her sexual harassment story.

In lieu of the evidence she had in her hand, she had a couple more questions for the captain. But once she got to his quarters, she found he wasn't there. When she bumped into the XO on the way to the bridge, he told her the captain had been called to the bridge.

She headed there, and as she was going to ascend the ladder she heard the sound of a helo. It was a large one and it hovered over the deck for only a few seconds before touching down.

She saw that the captain was on the flight deck waiting for the helo to land and she changed directions, making her way down to the flight deck. Her stomach dropped when she saw the official government emblem on the side of the helo.

When she reached the small knot of men hovering around a tall, distinguished man, Sia felt a jolt.

Senator Washington had landed on the deck of the

U.S.S. James McCloud, and from the determined look on his face, she could tell he wanted answers.

And he wanted them now.

Chapter 7

She approached the captain, and the steely brown eyes of the senator turned her way. "Is this the JAG handling the case?" he demanded.

"Sir," Sia said, reaching out a hand to him, but he just eyed her, the grief of his son's death plain in his eyes.

"I'm not here for a social visit, Commander. I'm here for who is responsible for my son's death. I've heard that it may not have been an accident."

"We do have some leads, sir. But our investigation is still ongoing and I don't—"

"You will brief me in fifteen minutes, Commander, in the captain's conference room."

"Sir."

"Is that a problem?"

"No, sir."

He indicated for the captain to show him the way,

and with a knowing look, he left with his entourage and the captain.

Scowling, Sia turned back to the interior of the ship. She needed to get back to Legal and talk to Chris before he was blindsided by the senator. He wouldn't be pleased to find out that she'd already had a run-in with him without Chris present. As the lead investigator, it was a responsibility he would consider his. If there was one thing she knew about Chris, it was that he wouldn't shirk this responsibility. She'd better get a move on and find him right away.

Sia headed back to the legal office. As she got to the top of the ladder, she felt two hands in the middle of her back. Before she could react, she was shoved violently. Losing her footing, she tumbled down the first three ladder steps before grabbing on to the handrail to stop herself from falling farther. Looking up, she caught a glimpse of something yellow ducking around the corner of the bulkhead.

"Ma'am. Are you all right?"

A seaman helped her to stand. Feeling shaky, Sia held on to the handrail until she felt more solid. "Can I escort you to sick bay, ma'am?"

"No, that won't be necessary, but thank you for your help." When she faced the young man, she recognized him from yesterday. "Oh, Ensign Brant. We talked yesterday in the Carrier Air Traffic Control Center."

"Yes, ma'am, I remember. I know how easy it is to fall. Takes some time to get used to the movement of a ship. When Lieutenant Cotes was training me..."

She grabbed his arm. The information he'd so innocently given her made her forget about her pain from the fall. "You replaced Lieutenant Cotes?"

Her reaction made his voice hesitate. "Yes, she went on to handling and I filled her vacancy."

Sia's hand tightened on his arm. "She's knowledgeable in radar systems?"

He looked down at her hand and up to her face. He nodded. "I'd say. She's a whiz."

"Thank you, Ensign. I appreciate your help."

This time she was sure she had been pushed and she was now sure she had herself a prime suspect, but that would have to wait until after she spoke to the senator. At least they had something solid to move the investigation forward. She was sure they would soon have a person in custody. Back at the legal office, she initiated contact with her legalman.

"McBride, how are you coming with that search for me on Master Chief Walker?"

His look was apologetic. "I got pulled off it, ma'am, by the captain, but I can get back to it tomorrow," he promised.

"Tomorrow?"

"It's almost closing time here. Remember, a six-hour difference."

"Of course. It's only morning here. If the captain tries to commandeer you again, tell him this is for the Washington case. He'll understand."

"Yes, ma'am."

Sia couldn't keep the excitement out of her voice. "I want you to extend that search for me. In fact, make it a priority over the master chief. Search previous billets for Lieutenant Susan Cotes, and I want to know about any pilot deaths, no matter what they are."

"Yes, ma'am. First thing tomorrow morning."

"You found something on Cotes?"

She turned to find Chris standing behind her and he sounded peeved. "Yes, when I searched Washington's rack, I discovered these."

Chris rifled through the pages and his head popped up, his eyes gleaming. "Typewritten notes from Cotes?"

"Yes, which means she was participating in this game they were playing and if the captain had talked to Washington, then he would have discovered her sexual harassment charge was bogus." The more evidence she gathered on this woman, the clearer it looked that she was the one they were looking for.

"She lied to us," Chris said, his voice a growl. "We'll need her back in here."

"The captain gave me the footage you requested." She pulled the flash drive out of her pocket. He took it out of her resisting fingers. "It would have been nice to know you requested access so I don't look like an idiot."

"Just like you withheld the autopsy from me?" He shot the words back at her like a bullet from a smoking gun.

She shrugged. "It's not the same thing."

He snorted. "Yes, it is. You admitted you still blame me. That's the real reason you're chafing at my control of this case. Admit it."

Sia brought up her arm to press her fingers against her suddenly throbbing temples. The man had a way of giving her a headache.

He grabbed her wrist. His eyes were stormy. "You're bleeding."

"What?" She looked at him as if she'd gone dumb.

"Your arm. You're bleeding. What happened?"

The concern in his eyes was genuine. After all they had been through and were still going through, Chris never changed. She felt the warmth of his body, the strength that poured effortlessly out of him, while he did nothing more than stand there. And she wanted to wrap herself in it, just for a moment or two, just long enough to draw strength from him and get her bearings back. But genuine or not, there was too much between them for a simple tug and hug. "I got pushed—again."

He scowled. "Then the first time was no accident."

She tried to get her wrist back, but he wouldn't let go. "No, it wasn't, and when I looked up I caught a glimpse of yellow."

His eyes flashed. "Like Cotes's yellow tunic?"

"Yes."

"Be careful, you're going to smear it all over your uniform." He pulled her over to a first-aid kit.

"You know, I can handle this myself," she said wryly.

He shrugged off her words and opened the kit, selecting a small, square package. Ripping it open, he unfolded the small pad inside. "It's in a hard-to-reach place on your forearm. I'll get it."

He wiped away the blood with the alcohol pad and it stung a bit. Sia went to pull away, but his grip was too strong. "What were you talking to McBride about?"

"I asked him to compile a list of all pilots who have died aboard the *McCloud*. Everything, including deaths ruled as accidents." He placed a bandage over the cut, his touch branding her with little licks of fire. "She lied about sending Washington notes and I discovered from Ensign Brant in air traffic control she was previously in that position and had been his training officer."

He raised his head from his work and looked at her, understanding dawning. "So she's familiar with radar."

The pain diminished to a dull throb now that the cut had been treated. Sia was happy to put some distance between them. "Yes, that's as far as I've gotten. I was going to look at her file more closely."

"We can do that now."

"No. That's going to have to wait," Sia said.

"Why?"

"Senator Washington is here and he wants to meet with us in the captain's conference room, now."

Chris sighed. "It's counterproductive for him to come here and demand answers when we haven't finished the investigation."

"We both know that. But he's grieving, Chris. We… we both know what that feels like. I can't say that I don't sympathize with him. In his shoes, I'd want answers, too."

"All right, but I want to come back here afterward and look up her file."

"We need to look at that footage, too, before we bring her back in here."

"Agreed. Can we agree on something else?"

"What's that?"

"You stick close to me or, at the very least, call for a master-at-arms if I'm not available or we have to split up?"

"All right. That's something I can agree to." When

they reached the conference room, Chris knocked on the door. The captain said, "Enter."

Sia and Chris walked through the door. The senator was sitting at the head of the table, his two aides on either side of him. One was working on a laptop and the other one was speaking to the senator in low tones.

Sia stood at attention until the captain asked her and Chris to sit down.

"I want to know what progress you've made on the investigation into my son's death. I can't sit in Washington anymore and get no report."

"Sir, as Commander Soto has told you, we are working on some solid leads."

"What are these leads? Did someone murder my boy?" His voice was authoritative, but underlined in raw sorrow.

Sia shifted uncomfortably. She remembered what had happened at the graveside when her father had verbally and physically attacked Chris. She knew he was remembering that day. He had to be.

She just hoped he didn't lose his cool, as he had back then.

She expected Chris to close down, to get tough, but instead his eyes went soft, filled with a knowing sympathy. "Sir, I know how you feel. I've been there. But at this time, we can't really reveal what we know because we haven't fully investigated what we have."

"You damn well will tell me what you know! You'll tell me now!" the senator bellowed.

When Chris didn't answer immediately, the senator rose. "Are you refusing to tell me what you know?"

"It's more complicated than that, sir."

"Complicated? Either someone killed my boy or not! There's nothing complicated about it and I want to know who it is."

Sia understood why Chris was being closemouthed about their leads. It wouldn't be conducive to the investigation if the obviously agitated senator went after Susan Cotes before they could question her.

"We have a suspect that we have identified."

Snarling, the senator rounded the table. Chris rose to face him. The senator jabbed at Chris's sternum hard with his forefinger. "I'm going to ask politely once more."

"Senator…"

"You stay out of this, Captain."

Sia rose, too, and stood shoulder to shoulder with Chris.

Chris's voice sliced the thick air like a lethal knife. "With all due respect, Senator Washington, that information will remain confidential until we have gathered all our evidence."

The senator, fueled by grief and anger, shoved Chris hard against the bulkhead. Both aides and the captain went to intervene, but Chris held up his hand to them. Softly he said, "I know what you're going through. But if you push this, you could ruin the investigation, taint our suspect and derail our interrogation. The suspect could walk. I know you want justice for Eli. That's what we want, too, and we'll do everything in our power to make it happen. We think Eli is worth that consideration and time. Do you?"

Everything inside the senator crumbled. The anger

that had cloaked him vanished, leaving him naked and vulnerable.

"I just want my boy back," he whispered. The captain ushered the shocked aides out of the conference room and shut the door behind him.

Sia put a hand on the senator's arm. His face crumpled and tears ran down his face. Sia's heart squeezed tight and she wrapped her arms around the inconsolable man.

Her eyes met Chris's over the senator's shoulder. He was the one she wanted to hold. The bleak look in his eyes told her that keeping information from the senator about his son's possible killer had taken a toll. But the courage and the skillful way he'd defused the situation made her heart catch in her chest. Hollis surely had been right.

It only made Sia more ashamed of how she'd treated him six years ago.

After seeing the senator to the helo and assuring him that he would have answers soon, Chris and Sia watched him take off. They headed back to the legal office, but found Billy had a few people inside that made it a bit crowded. Since Chris was bunking with a roommate, Sia suggested they go to her stateroom.

Once inside, Sia booted up her computer to check for emails. "Nothing from him yet." She looked at her watch. "Oh, damn. He's probably gone home. I'll check with him tomorrow. Let's review the footage."

Sia plugged the flash drive into her computer and started the file. They watched as the jets approached. It was easy to see which plane was Monroe's and which one was Washington's. It was clear the second plane's pilot was in distress. Monroe landed his craft without incident, just as he'd said.

"Washington is flying too low," Chris said. He watched closely as the jet clipped the edge of the ship and skidded.

As she watched Sia couldn't help thinking about her brother. How it must have been for him at the end. Seeing the crash also made her think of Chris. How it had been for him when his jet had collided with her brother's. Tears gathered in her eyes and she quickly brushed them away. She minimized the footage.

She looked at Chris, but instead of the emotion she expected to see, he looked puzzled and unsettled. She replayed the footage and paused it just as the jets came alongside each other, their wings almost touching.

She could almost imagine the plane on the right was her brother's and the one on the left Chris's. She could also imagine how they must have collided.

Back then it had seemed cut-and-dried. Pilot error. But now in light of the two pilot deaths, Sia wasn't so sure anymore.

Chris snapped out of his reverie and stared at her. His eyes sharpened. He reached out and touched her cheek with the back of his hand, wiping away the telltale tears.

He looked at the computer and gently closed it. The image of the jets winked out.

He wondered if his heart could take any more. If he could, as he had said so many times, move past this source of pain and guilt in his past, in her past. He wanted to let loose the feelings that were still locked up in his heart, but he was afraid of the consequences of her rejection.

And the sight of those two jets so close in the air. Milliseconds away from disaster. Facing death each time he jumped into his cockpit had been easier.

Easier than looking into Sia's eyes and seeing her pain, her loss, seeing that she was holding on to something so desperately her knuckles were turning white. And deep down it hurt that she needed his exoneration, needed to have a reason to believe he wasn't to blame for Rafael's death.

And sometimes, he wondered if it really mattered. Rafael was dead. Dead and gone. But they were here, warm, living flesh. He wanted her. As unreasonable as it might seem, he wanted her. Still.

He went to pull his hand away, not sure if he could offer her any comfort she would accept. When her hand quickly rose to curl around his, his heart twisted with a painful longing that had multiplied for six long years.

"Don't," she said softly.

He could feel the tremors in her as the tears fell freely from her eyes and he wasn't sure if they were now for Rafael or for all they had lost.

Her hand rose along his arm, to his shoulder as she leaned in closer to him. With a soft, low cry, her trembling lips met his, and then covered them, moving gently, sweetly.

Chris was drowning in hunger, fighting a need that rose swiftly, was banked ruthlessly. He didn't want her to just react to him. A ragged sense of honor kept him motionless when instinct dictated he haul her into his arms. It was the memory of the pain in her eyes only a moment ago that kept him from giving in to those urges, that had shouted clearer than words that she was still conflicted about him.

Her mouth moved to his jaw, and he clenched it, hard, when her lips dragged over the stubble. His lungs dragged in the scent of her in a guilty, greedy swallow, and his muscles quivered with the force of his control.

She didn't need this. The thought hammered in his head, keeping rhythm with the pulse in his veins. He didn't know what drove her, but he knew she was vulnerable in a way she hadn't allowed herself in a long time. Knew that even her well-worn defenses must have limits.

And, he had to admit, so did his.

And he was equally certain given time they'd be firmly back in place. She was still reeling from all the memories this case had brought back and adding him to the mix only made it more complicated. He tried to remember that as she caught his bottom lip between her teeth, bit down gently. He had to admit this would be folly for both of them. Keeping their relationship professional was the wiser choice, but where Sia was concerned he seemed to lose his focus, set aside his own pain. But there'd been emotion in her answer, in just that single word. And it was apparent in her kiss. Each touch crumbled his control a bit further.

Her fingers skimmed over his chest. His muscles jumped beneath her touch, quivering. His hands went to her hips, intending to put her away from him. In a moment. This must be a special kind of hell reserved just for him, for offenses committed.

When her mouth touched his again, his arms slipped

around her waist, and he kissed her back with a crushing desire that should have worried her. Should have had her pulling away. Instead it served to scorch them both.

His fingers tunneled in her hair and he held her head still, consumed her mouth. And he imagined just for a moment what it would be like to make love to her without fearing the inevitable moment when her defenses would snap back into place. Keeping him out and the memories locked away.

No barriers existed between them now. The certainty shimmered between them, tempted with a heated promise. And the knowledge was sweet, perhaps made more because he knew how rare the moment was.

He could feel her heart race, keeping pace with his. His tongue pressed at her lips for entrance, and they parted in a provocative way that made him groan. He dragged her closer, one hand sliding beneath her serviceable khaki shirt, skimming over her smooth back. She arched against him, and the last remnant of his control gave way under the weight of his need for her.

After so many years apart, he took his time, reveled in the freedom to touch and savor her. He snagged the hem of her shirt, drew it over her head. Skin against skin, warm and vibrant, made him unravel a bit more. The silk of her bra against his chest was sensual, charging his blood to a torrent. The smooth skin of her shoulder beckoned his mouth, his muscles tense. Breathing hard, he paused to get the surging passion under control.

The bunk was close enough that he could add just the right amount of pressure. They would end up where he wanted her, where he could explore her to his satisfaction, every inch of their bodies touching. They could give their passion free rein, forget all thoughts, all doubts.

He bent, scooped her up in his arms and laid her on the bunk. When he followed her down, it was with passion held in check, and something far more dangerous rising to the surface. He loomed half over her, tangled his hands in her long, curly tresses, rubbing the strands against the sensitive pads of his fingers, moving the mass away from her striking face. An aching path of tenderness carved through him. Her bruises were like a badge of courage against her golden skin, a reminder that life was so fleeting. His lips brushed over the marred skin, one warrior paying homage to another.

Sia froze under his soft mouth, aware that something had shifted in his rhythm. Uncertain of her response, she felt his mouth move to the places on her body where she'd been hurt, sensually identifying each of her injuries, soothing each. His tenderness made the myriad of emotions locked inside her clamor for release. Again he was offering her something she didn't know how to accept, or return. She only knew he tangled her emotions into unidentifiable knots. Wreaked havoc on her system. The minutes stretched, encased in silver.

Chris took his time relearning the contours of Sia's body, saw her eyes, glazed but wary. And understanding rocked him, so sudden and hard he shivered with the knowledge. Walls worked both ways. Barriers were erected and served to protect what was inside, but also worked to keep everything out. He wondered if she knew his defenses seemed to be made of sand.

Their mouths collided, tongues tangled. Passion still sluiced through his veins, but tempered for the moment.

He teased her with supple, lingering kisses as his hands played on her flesh, languid and dreamy. And when he felt her body soften against his, heard her breath hitch slightly, he knew this was what he craved. What he'd always craved. To feel her melt with bliss. To feel her hands frantic on his flesh. To know with every gasp and moan he drew from her she thought of him. Only him.

His hands drifted over her breasts, impatient with the silk barrier. Deftly he reached behind her and released the clasp. Freed, the soft globes gleamed in the light, tipped with tight pink nipples.

His fingers circled one nipple, flicking it with his thumb. Her breath hissed in and she reached for him, her fingers clutching his shoulders, skating over his chest. A thousand points of flame burst beneath his skin, and she pulled his head down to her. With a soft moan of pleasure, he drew her proffered nipple into his mouth, savagely satisfied to hear his name tumble from her lips. Cupping her other breast in his hand, he fondled it until dual assault had her body twisting against him.

A haze seemed to have formed over all thought, all reason. There was only Sia, her flavor tracing through his system, her scent embedded in his senses. Light from the single lamp in the stateroom slanted across them, illuminating their skin and making it glow. Her fingers were fumbling with his pants, and each slight brush of her knuckles against his abdomen was the most exquisite form of torture.

Desire rushed through him, made a mockery of his control. Stepping away, only a fraction, he stripped the cloth barrier away from his body and kicked it away. He donned protection and pulled her to face him until they lay together, side to side, so that every inch of their bodies touched. Finding the pulse at the base of her throat, he stroked it with his tongue. Restlessly, she drew her leg sensuously up the length of his leg and across his hip.

His breath heaved out of his lungs. The time had passed for slow and easy. His hand kneaded the satin of her thigh, felt the whisper of muscle beneath the silky skin. It was always an erotic delight to rediscover Sia's softness. His fingers trailed closer to her core of heat, and he thrilled as her body twisted with need.

She forgot to breathe. He gave her no choice but to feel. Sia gloried in the choice, even realizing it came with risk. But right now there was only his body close to hers, smooth flesh stretched over padded muscle. Her fingers traced over him, where sinew and bone joined to leave intriguing hollows. Each begged to be explored with soft lips and swift hands.

Longing battled with doubt. He traced the crease where her leg met her hip and she stiffened, her lungs clogged. He was moving down her body, painting flesh with his tongue. Her blood turned hot, molten, and chugged through her veins like lava. Her world, her focus, narrowed to include only the two of them.

Need, Chris was finding, was a double-edged sword, one as painful as it was pleasurable. And, poised on that razor-edged peak, he was as primed as she for a fall. He couldn't find it in himself to care. His mouth found her moist warmth and her back arched. He slipped his hands beneath her hips, lifted her to devour. The soft, strangled sounds tumbling from her lips urged him on, to take more. To give more. And when she shot to re-lease in a wild shuddering mass, she cried his name.

Sia fought to haul breath into her lungs. Her limbs were like liquid. And for the moment at least, she felt utterly tranquil. She felt the bunk move, and her eyelids fluttered open. Tranquility abruptly fled. Here was the danger she'd forgotten, in the primal masculine man bending over her. Her hand rose of its own volition, curved around his neck and brought his mouth to hers.

His breath heaved out of his chest as her teeth scored his skin lightly, nipping a path from his shoulder to his belly. His restraint unraveled a bit more with each soft touch.

The light illuminated their thrashing bodies, spill-ing on the bunk. Chris's gentleness had vanished, hun-ger raging. His vision misted, but his other senses were alert. Achingly so. The sweet, dark flavor of her tongue battling with his. The silkiness of her hair brushing against his skin and the sexy, tight grasp of her hands as she explored him where he was hot, hard and pulsing.

The teasing was gone. Gentleness was beyond him. His arousal was primal, basic and immediate. His hands battled hers, and he rolled her to his side, drew her leg over his hips. Testing her readiness with one finger, he watched her eyes, shadows of emotion and desire mov-ing through the soft, dewy brown like comets.

He moved into position, his shaft barely parting her warm cleft, and stilled. He eased into her, her eyes di-rectly on his, now bare and vulnerable, opening more than just her body to him. She twisted and moaned against him as he moved in tiny increments, not satis-fied until he was seated deep inside her. Then he took her mouth with his own, savagely aware every inch of their bodies was touching. Inside and out. And still it wasn't enough.

He withdrew from her only to lunge again, each time deeper, harder, faster. They were caught in a vortex, spinning wilder and wilder. Out of control. He saw her face spasm, felt the clench of her inner muscles, swallowed her cry with his mouth. And then, only then did he let the tide sweep him under and dash him up and over the edge.

Minutes, or hours, later he stroked a hand along the curve of her waist before settling it possessively on her hip. Each beat of her heart echoed with his. Their breathing slowed, and eventually reason intruded. He started to move away and her fingers tightened in an automatic reflexive response. Reluctantly he ignored it. The protection he'd used was fast losing its effectiveness. He took care of it and rolled back to her. To please himself, he pushed the heavy tangle of her hair away from her face and skimmed his fingertips over her shoulder and down her arm.

It would be easy to stay like this, to cuddle and make love, but they were much more than simply lovers. He knew from personal experience it would be wonderful to fall asleep cradled in her arms.

Once before he'd thought they'd forged a bond, until Sia had ruthlessly cut him out of her life and the distance had yawned between them like a deep chasm. He wasn't going to make that mistake again. She would have to come to terms with him, and that was something he couldn't help her with.

Sia could see the change in his eyes and she hated

the emotions and the feelings locked up inside her. The sheer satisfaction of being this intimate with Chris was something she cherished, but the past hung between them like a specter. "We both know this doesn't settle anything, it only makes it more convoluted and complicated. Until we work through our past, it'll be the white elephant in the room. Is that something you want, Sia?"

He picked up her hand and measured it against his. She could see the emotions dance like flame in his eyes. Without conscious volition, her fingers locked with his. He couldn't know what he was asking. She wanted to get past it all, but she couldn't. She didn't have answers yet. Even as she mourned their relationship and all they had lost, she felt locked in her decision.

She hated this. Trying to quench the lick of panic in her veins, she moved closer to him. She didn't want to deal with the jumble of emotions, the mingled doubts and fears. Far better to end this now. Again. Before there was a sticky tangle of recriminations and disappointments to assuage.

But as he drew her chin up to meet his eyes, she couldn't, so she changed the subject. "What was it about Washington's accident that bothered you?"

It took him a moment to change gears and she could see the disappointment in his eyes, but he let it go for now. It was just a reprieve. She knew that. Maybe when she had to make a final decision about Chris, she would have more answers.

"I don't know. I can't put my finger on it. But something about his landing is bothering me. It's been a while since I landed on a carrier at night."

"It'll come to you. Try not to think about it too hard."

He nodded.

Sia slipped out of the bunk, unabashed about her nakedness. It fueled her to know Chris was looking and admiring. She pulled a T-shirt and shorts out of her locker and put them on. Her dark hair obscured her vision of Chris lying on his side in the bunk watching her. With a small smile, she scooped up her laptop and opened it. When it woke, the screen was still on the jets. With a pang, Sia minimized it. "As soon as McBride finishes with that research, I'm sure we'll find Cotes was aboard the *McCloud* when Rafael died."

"Sia, it's best to draw conclusions only when we have evidence that is the case."

"That's true, but I have a feeling about this. It's going to clear his name. I just know it."

Chris hadn't moved from the bunk, nor had he donned any clothes. The sheet was draped over his groin, but his well-muscled chest and every other part of his fine body was displayed. It was hard for her to concentrate.

"Investigations aren't about feelings. Don't let your emotions override your logic," he said as he shifted with a ripple of muscle to his side to pillow his head on his arm.

"I'm not. I'm just stating what I think is the truth. Why are you being so negative? Don't you want to be exonerated?"

He sat up, his face pulling into a frown. "I lost everything that was important to me six years ago, Sia. I've made a new life and moved on. But I can see that you haven't. We can't live in the past."

Sia stood and came over to the bunk. "I know that.

But this isn't about moving on. This is about justice for my brother. Justice for you. If someone tampered with your radar or drugged you, then it's our duty to bring that person to justice. There is no statute of limitations on murder!"

"Sia," he said, grabbing her hand when she went to turn away, "I know you want this more than anything, but you have to be prepared for whatever the truth is going to reveal. I don't want you to set yourself up for disappointment."

She extricated her hand from his. Her overloaded senses only distracted her from her anger. "Maybe this doesn't mean as much to you as it does to me. I'll never stop trying to prove my brother wasn't at fault that day. I just don't believe it."

"But it's easy for you to believe I was. To blame me. You and your family ostracized me. I was already handling a load of guilt, yet I couldn't even get any peace at Rafael's funeral. Your father attacked me."

"He was hurting. He wanted someone to blame."

"And you sided with them," he said, his voice harsh and raw.

"They were my family."

"You said you loved me, Sia. Doesn't that mean anything to you?"

"Yes, it does. But I couldn't go against my family."

"No, because you wanted someone to blame, too."

The air crackled between them and Sia's eyes flared with emotion and anger. "I wanted to support my family, Chris. That is the bottom line. My parents were devastated. My father turned to the bottle and my mother lost her will. I saw her lose the battle with living every day."

"How are they now? Have they moved past—?"

"You don't know? They didn't move past it, Chris. They died five years ago in a car crash because my father was drunk."

Chapter 8

Chris lay quietly, listening to his roommate complete his morning ritual. It was dark in the stateroom except for the dim lights over his bunk. Chris guessed it was only about four o'clock or four-thirty.

He turned over until he faced the wall. Sleep had been elusive and fitful since he left Sia's cabin. His shock at the news of her parents' deaths had hit him very hard, right in his heart.

His loss was now totally complete. Unequivocally permanent.

And he had to wonder. He didn't want to complete the thought, but he wasn't easy, even on himself. Did she blame him for her parents' deaths as well as her brother's? The thought gnawed at him in a place that, even after six years, was still raw. And he had to assume some of the blame. He was indirectly responsible for their deaths. It was his error that killed Rafe.

Being with her again had brought it all back. He didn't have to hear her tell him she couldn't forgive him when forgiveness was what he wanted and needed. He knew she couldn't and that reality shattered his foundations even more.

Like a thirsty man so close to water he could smell it, but wasn't allowed to drink.

He would have been kidding himself if he'd thought there had been any way back into their good graces. The Sotos had cut him out of their lives as ruthlessly as his own father had, but for a short time, he'd had it all. The love of his life, a family who loved him like he was their own and a best friend who had brought all his dreams and hopes together in one neat package.

It had been fleeting, but it had been real, for as long as it had lasted.

Unable to fall asleep, he donned his running gear and slipped out of the ship to the flight deck. It was quiet this morning and almost completely devoid of people.

There was a lone runner and he swore softly. He'd told her it wasn't safe for her to be on her own, but independent Sia didn't think anything of running early in the morning without an escort and he was the last person she wanted to see.

It took him a few lengthy strides to catch up with her. They ran side by side in silence until the sun came up over the horizon.

"I'm sorry about your parents," he said softly, not looking at her. He kept his gaze straight ahead on the pink horizon.

Sia slowed to a walk, not looking at him at first, as if

she was processing all that had happened. He reached out and touched her arm, so she looked over at him.

She held his gaze for a fraction of a second longer, and then dipped her chin, before coming to a complete stop. "I'm sorry, too. I miss them."

"I miss them, too," he said simply and it seemed to be enough. She nodded and squeezed his arm.

"Since I couldn't sleep, I've been thinking about Lieutenant Cotes. She had motivation and means, but did she have the opportunity?" Sia lunged into a calf stretch on first one leg, then the other.

Before Chris could respond, a female voice interrupted.

"Excuse me, sir."

Chris turned to find a tall blond woman approaching them. She was dressed in red, marking her as one of the flight crew. As she got closer, he realized she wasn't as young as he'd first thought. She had a long scar from her temple down to her chin. It was an old scar that had faded with age. Something about the scar stirred a memory, but one that eluded him.

"Special Agent Vargas," she shielded her eyes from the rising sun.

"Yes, and this is Lieutenant Commander Soto."

"Ma'am." The woman nodded her hello. "I was directed to you by the XO. I was meeting with him on the bridge when we saw you running on the flight deck."

"You are?" Sia asked.

"Lieutenant Maria Jackson. I'm one of the landing signal officers and I was on the flight deck when Lieutenant Washington lost control of his jet and skidded.

In fact, I was the one handling the meatball and directing him in."

"We talked with several crew members and watched footage of the crash. If we come up with more questions, we'll be sure to talk to you." Chris didn't see any need to rehash what had happened on deck. They had the footage and had interviewed both Washington's wingman and the air boss.

The woman's gaze narrowed. When he tried to go around her, she moved to block his path. Something flashed in her eyes, something menacing and chilling, but it was quickly gone and Chris had to question whether he'd seen anything at all or if it was a trick of the light.

"Actually," she said impatiently, "I'm not here about what happened on deck that night. I'm here about what happened before Lieutenant Washington crashed."

"What is that?" Sia asked. Standing beside the tall woman, Sia seemed even more fragile.

Maria looked pensive for a moment. "I didn't really think anything about it until today when the XO mentioned you were investigating Susan and if I had any information regarding her and Lieutenant Washington, I should report to you."

"And what do you have to say about Lieutenant Cotes?" Chris prompted.

"She likes to play games with men," she said derisively, not looking away. "I've seen it in the past. With Lieutenant Washington, it was just more of the same. The argument started in the wardroom. When he walked away, she followed him. She continued the dispute with him right near his fighter. She had a piece of paper in her hand and she was waving it around. He was shaking his head and I could tell he was angry."

"Do you know what they were arguing about?" Sia asked.

"Not completely." The woman lowered her voice. "But she made a threat."

Chris regarded her for a moment, and then said, "What kind of threat?"

Her tone ominous, she replied, "That he would regret it if he didn't stop harassing her. She would put a stop to it. I just assumed she would go to the captain, but I'm not sure now what she really meant."

"Now?" Sia asked.

Maria shrugged. "Well, now that he's dead."

"She was near his plane, you said." Looked like they had more to interrogate Susan Cotes about than just the notes and her knowledge of radar. The evidence was mounting.

"That's right. And he stalked away when she made her threat."

"What did she do?"

Maria looked uncomfortable, but resigned to the onerous task of informing on a friend. "She ducked under the plane and I lost track of her. I had to prepare the deck for a landing, so I got busy. It was only after the crash and the XO's information that I thought of it."

"Would she have had access to his radar equipment from underneath the plane?" Sia asked.

"Sure, she could have. I didn't see her, but it's possible."

"Thank you for your time, Lieutenant Jackson," Sia said.

She nodded and walked away.

"Looks like she had opportunity, too," Chris said.

"Looks like it. Let's get her back into interrogation."

Chris nodded. "Let's get cleaned—"

The sound of a shot echoed across the deck. Chris pushed Sia toward the cover of two jets and several more shots rang out. One plinked into the nearest jet, much too close to Sia's head. Chris pushed her down and covered her. She started to protest, but he shushed her. He heard the sound of running feet and the clank of a metal door somewhere above them. Then silence.

He lifted himself off her and looked down into her face. She was flushed with fear, her pupils dilated. He cursed that he hadn't been carrying his sidearm on the deck. He'd left it in his locker. From now on he was going to carry it. He saw the captain approaching with angry strides.

"Are you all right?" he said, checking her over himself.

"Yes. I'm fine. Who is shooting at us on an aircraft carrier?"

"That's what I would like to know." The captain's voice was filled with anger.

A half an hour later in the captain's conference room, Sia and Chris sat at a long brown table.

"All the sidearms that were signed out of the armory are accounted for. None of them have been fired."

"Someone could have smuggled one aboard. I sent the bullets we pried out of the fuselage of the two jets to my forensics specialist at Hickam. Once we find the weapon, he can match the ballistics."

"The only other sidearm that is aboard this ship," Sia said, "is yours."

"Mine is locked up in my stateroom inside my locker."

"It wouldn't hurt to check it, Vargas," the captain said. "We will be getting underway today. Heading back to San Diego for a few more extensive repairs to the carrier. I want whoever is responsible for what's going on caught before we dock. Is that clear?"

The captain pulled open the door and signaled a master-at-arms, the Navy's version of the MP. "I want you to secure Lieutenant Cotes in Legal until Special Agent Vargas and Commander Soto arrive. Then I want you to wait outside for further instructions."

The steely-eyed man nodded and left.

"Why don't you two get cleaned up and conduct a thorough interrogation of Lieutenant Cotes and check your weapon, Vargas. Report back to me with your findings. You're both dismissed. I have a call to make to Senator Washington. Get me some answers and the perpetrator."

When Sia started to walk back to her cabin, Chris followed.

"Where are you going?"

"With you."

"Why?"

"Someone shot at us. You were pushed down the ladder. Not leaving you alone."

"Suit yourself."

She walked down the gangway and navigated the ladders, favoring her recently injured arm, but Chris could see the way her hand trembled on the rail. When they got to her cabin, she reached for the handle and turned it. He touched her arm and she stilled.

Some color was returning to her cheeks. But he remembered how she had looked after the gunshots. She'd been pasty-white and, despite her surprising mettle during the incident, looked like a feather could knock her over.

"I'm fine," she said, her voice catching as he caressed her arm.

"That's good bravado, Commander, but I'm not buying it." He turned her around and cupped her face. Her skin was smooth, soft and warm against his palms. The feel of her calmed something a bit wild inside him.

"Buying what?"

He tilted his head and stared at her. "I've been shot at before. I can lay a bet you never have."

"No. I won't take that wager and it doesn't mean I'm going to back down, either."

"I wouldn't bet against that."

"Good, because you'd lose."

"I won't let anything happen to you," he said, his voice a shade rougher now. He leaned in and pressed his forehead to hers. With his face close to hers, their gazes locked.

"I'm a JAG officer. I'm expected to take care of myself, but this time, I'll take you up on that. You're the one with the gun."

He pulled her into his arms, tucked her against his chest. "And I know how to use it."

"That doesn't surprise me. You have many skills."

He leaned back enough so he could look into her face. "Oh, do I?"

She smiled. The beauty of it caught him off guard. It was the first genuine smile he'd seen on her since he met her at JAG. He liked the softness of it, the vulnerability. It made his heart ache. It gave him hope where there was none, a hope he wasn't sure he could handle.

It was natural for his head to drop, his mouth to home in on hers. It felt right and good when his lips covered her soft smiling ones. And when she softened rather than stiffened beneath his hands and mouth, he gave up any pretense of trying to control himself where she was concerned.

The past and the present were so tangled up in his head and in his heart, he didn't even try to convince himself he knew the difference anymore. He wanted to think he was well past that part of his life. Clearly, he was not, when it came to the one woman he'd never been able to forget.

"If we didn't have work to do…"

She sighed. "Duty calls. It always does and in this case, we have to answer. It's too important not to."

He nodded. When she opened the door, he crowded in after her.

"What are you doing?" She put her hand on his chest to stop him.

"I said I wasn't leaving you." He pushed forward, liking the way her hand felt against him.

"Chris, I'll lock the door," she said, and couldn't help the small smile that lessened her outraged tone.

He smiled back. "That's a good idea, but I'm going to be on this side of it."

"Oh, for the…all right," she said, giving in after taking a look at his face. "But you stay on the other side of the head door."

"I will."

Inside, Sia grabbed her uniform and disappeared into the head. He heard the shower come on as he imagined her getting in under the spray. All that glorious skin wet and gleaming. When the water went off, he shifted and sighed in relief.

"Oh, shoot," he heard her say in distress.

"You okay?"

"I…ah…forgot my underwear. Could you…" She trailed off.

Chris chuckled.

"It's not funny!"

"Oh, it's providing me with great amusement."

"I was in too much of a hurry to get away from you."

"Right." He went to her locker and opened it. "Does it matter…"

"No! Just grab a pair, for God's sake."

He picked out one from all the lacy numbers in her locker and hooked it to his forefinger. He knocked on the door.

She opened it, a towel wrapped around her, her shoulders looking damp and inviting. Her face was mortified when she saw the panties dangling from his finger. She snatched them away and slammed the door.

He chuckled again.

"You'd think an NCIS agent would have better manners," she shouted through the door.

He laughed. "We're a coarse bunch of SOBs. Most of us come from a law enforcement background, the rest from the military."

"I have to say I was surprised you went into the agency. I thought you'd still be flying." Her voice was subdued now, but filled with curiosity.

"I resigned my commission shortly after you left for New York. I tried to kill myself with alcohol for the first month. I'd probably still be there or in the ground."

"What happened?" He didn't miss the anguish in her voice and it made his gut clench at the memories of the worst time in his life.

"A buddy called and he hauled me out of my apartment and read me the riot act."

"Sounds like a good friend."

"He is. He worked for NCIS and encouraged me to apply. I thought it sounded like I could make a difference."

She opened the door. "And have you?"

She looked scrubbed and fresh, her hair pulled back and securely fastened.

"I think so. The work is rewarding, but tough. I used the long hours like I did alcohol. It dulled the pain and after a while it got better."

She put her hand on his chest, her eyes clear and looking deep into his. "That's good, Chris."

Her sympathy made him want to draw her close, but he was aware of the time and their responsibilities. It was the only thing that stopped him.

"Time for my shower," he said, meeting her gaze head-on.

She grabbed her hat and nodded she was ready to go.

Back in his own stateroom, he opened his locker and pulled out his weapon. Sia looked over his shoulder.

"Your gun is here."

It looked the same as when he'd left it. He nodded. He caught a whiff of cleaning oil and noticed his kit was just below the weapon. Reaching down, he opened it. Nothing inside was disturbed. He called the captain and gave him that information while Sia took a seat on his bunk.

While he was in the shower, he mentally went over what they knew. Two aviators were dead. It seemed both of them had had radar issues and both of them had been incoherent at the end. They had a dead master chief who'd tried to murder Sia. Two planes were being thoroughly investigated. Last but not least, an LSO who had seen the suspect under one of the jets.

They needed more answers. When he emerged from the head, they headed to the legal office.

"Your weapon is still in your locker?" Sia asked, her gaze flowing over him like a warm caress.

He was sure it was involuntary, but that thought did nothing to lessen the impact of her eyes on him. "Right now, I have it against the small of my back. I'm not taking any more chances."

She looked pensive. "So someone must have smuggled the weapon aboard."

He reached up and rubbed her shoulder to tell her he would stick by her. "Looks like it."

Two masters-at-arms were standing on either side of the door as Sia and Chris approached. The guards nodded as Chris opened the door and indicated for Sia to enter.

Lieutenant Cotes was sitting at the small interrogation table. Her hands were nervously intertwining, but ceased when they entered.

Sia sat and Chris nestled in next to her. Sia pulled Lieutenant Cotes's file out of her briefcase.

"We have received information you and Lieutenant Washington had an argument on the flight deck the night before he flew his mission," Sia said.

Chris was beginning to think Sia would make an excellent cop. Her interrogation skills were very good. She didn't elaborate or expound on what she was saying. She just gave her suspect a little rope.

Susan shifted and looked away, her lips tightening. "It's true. We had an argument, but I only wanted to talk to him and tell him I was going to the captain because his notes hadn't stopped."

"What was his response?" Sia said, her eyes sharp.

"He got really angry and accused *me* of playing games and said I didn't need to bother because he was going to talk to the captain." She dropped her head in her hands. "This is a nightmare. Nothing good comes from even speaking to a pilot."

"Were you?"

"Was I what?" Susan asked, her head coming up, her eyes moist.

"Were you playing games?" Sia elaborated, her voice even.

"No!" Susan snapped.

Sia arched a brow and studied her so hard that Susan dropped her hands to her lap and glanced away. Without a word, she pulled out the notes she had found in Washington's bunk and laid them out on the table one by one.

Susan's eyes swung suspiciously toward the pieces of paper, and then her face went white as she studied the notes. Color flushed back into her cheeks as her shocked and angry eyes met Sia's. "I didn't write these. I don't know what kind of game Lieutenant Washington was playing, but I wasn't a part of it."

Chris said softly, "Did you tamper with Lieutenant Washington's jet?"

"No! I told you. We fought on the deck, but I left when he did. I didn't touch the plane. I had nothing to do with his death!" She smacked the table with the flat of her hand.

Sia ignored the outburst and fired off another question. "Where were you at zero one hundred hours yesterday?"

"In my bunk sleeping after my shift," Susan said, clearly wondering where this was heading. "Why?"

"Someone with a yellow tunic pushed me down the ladder."

"It wasn't me," she said, even more agitated.

"Can anyone confirm you were there…sleeping?"

Susan's eyes narrowed and her mouth tightened. "No. I don't know. As I said, I was sleeping."

"What about your roommate?"

"She was on duty."

"I have one more question for you. Do you own a gun?"

Susan made a soft sound and looked away. "No, I don't own a gun."

"Have you fired one recently?"

"What? At you and Agent Vargas? Is that what you're asking?"

"Have you?"

"No! All the answers to your questions are no!"

Chris's phone buzzed and when he looked down, he

saw he had a text from Math. He checked the message. *Need to talk to you now.*

"Looks like Math has something for us." Chris got up and opened the door. "Lieutenant Cotes, you may go back to your duty station."

Susan angrily pushed her chair back and with a sullen look on her face brushed past them. Chris shut the door.

"I'll commission us a vehicle and we'll head over to Hickam to talk to Math."

An hour later they were in the procured vehicle and heading over to the base. Chris navigated the streets easily.

"Your old stomping grounds?" Sia asked.

"Yes, we docked here often. I will say that Rafe and I took advantage of the beaches and the pretty women in bikinis."

Sia smiled. "Rafe was my brother, but he was purely male."

After getting through security, they were directed to a hangar on the north side of the base. Chris pulled up to the large gray structure and he and Sia left the car.

Once inside, they found Math examining a large piece of what looked like the fuselage of a fighter.

"Math?"

Math turned around and smiled. "Hey, that was fast."

"The ship is docked less than a mile from here. It took longer to get a car. The Navy and their red tape."

"Hello, pretty Sia."

Sia smiled at him and shook his hand.

"What do you have for us?" Chris said.

Math rubbed at his tired eyes, went over to a desk

and sat down. He indicated two chairs. Sia and Chris settled in.

"What is it?"

"I went over the planes and can tell you there were no structural issues. Both of them were sound, solid pieces of machinery. However, I can't say the same thing about each radar. Both of them were damaged."

"From the impact or from something else?" Chris asked, leaning forward.

"It would be hard to determine. Saunders's jet took less damage when it crashed into the ocean. According to the data recovered from the flight recorder, it was clear he was at the controls most of the way down, so he tried to minimize the damage when he realized he was about to crash."

"Realized? What do you mean?" Sia asked.

"I can only guess that he was in and out of consciousness most of the descent. I think he was unaware his jet was so close to the water. He made no move to adjust his controls between the time of the collision and just before he hit the water."

"He was mentally incapacitated?" she said, giving Chris a knowing look.

"He was most likely mentally and physically incapacitated. Whether it was from something inherent or introduced into his system, the ME has to make that determination."

"There was no conclusive evidence from his autopsy that indicates he was drugged," Sia said, and she looked triumphant that her insistence that a drug had been involved in the pilot deaths had turned out to be true.

"Well, I suggest the ME take another look. That pilot

was not acting normal when handling that jet. It took a long time for him to crash. Several minutes."

"It's true," Sia said. "His wingman confirmed that."

"And the flight recorder corroborates the wingman's testimony."

"Did he have water in his lungs?" Math asked, his brow furrowing in thought.

"According to the report, yes. He drowned," Chris replied, thinking Sia was right and they did have a drugging of a military pilot on a U.S. carrier.

Math nodded in confirmation. "Then he was alive for some time after he hit the water."

"So he had ample time to eject?" Sia said, her eyes shining a bit.

"More than ample time," Math said.

"And Washington's jet?" Chris needed to know if the same things added up there.

Math reached up and scratched his stubbled jaw. "There it is cut-and-dried. The radar was damaged when the jet hit the ship and exploded. It had more extensive damage."

"So then you can't tell if it was tampered with?" Sia said, disappointment evident in her tone. They were both hoping for some kind of evidence they could use.

Math grinned and cocked his head. "On the contrary, I can."

"What did you find?" Chris knew that look. Math had it whenever he'd found something substantial. Chris always liked that look.

"Two fingerprints. I ran them through AFIS and I got a hit."

"Who do they belong to?" Chris said, anticipation curling in his gut.

"Lieutenant Susan Cotes."

Chapter 9

"Chris, I do want to point out to you the fingerprints I lifted off the casing were almost perfect."

"No smudges? No smears?"

"None. But the evidence speaks for itself. Your case is solved thanks to me and I did it in just under twenty-four hours." Math smirked.

"It would seem so."

Sia and Chris made their way back to the ship. Chris reported to the captain and got permission to bring Susan Cotes back to the interrogation. She paced restlessly in her stateroom as Chris entered. "Are you all right?"

"Yes," she said. "I want the truth from that woman."

"Let's go get it."

Sia nodded, her face solemn. Chris headed toward the door, and just as she was going to shut down her laptop, her email notification dinged. She clicked on the icon and her email message popped up. The email was from her aide. He'd gotten the list she wanted of all pilot deaths aboard Navy ships from the time her brother had been killed. She clicked on the list and found eight names, including Rafael's. She also noticed her aide had included pictures. In the email, he said it was important she open the file. She clicked on the attachment. The file loaded and she gasped softly.

"Chris," Sia said, her eyes on her computer screen.

Chris paused with his hand on the door handle. "What is it?"

"Look at this."

When he walked closer to the screen, he swore softly under his breath.

"They look like you. Well, except for Rafael. All of them, including Saunders and Washington. They look enough like you to be brothers.

"Susan Cotes is a serial killer. It's clear from these photos." She was reeling from this information, not quite sure how she should feel. Not quite sure how she should act. If Chris had been targeted by a serial killer all those years ago, then her brother had been nothing more than collateral damage.

And, Chris…Chris had been the intended victim.

Her stomach churned at this news, and in the bright light of day she had to realize she had been so off-base. It was true the *accident* that had taken her brother's life was no accident at all. It was supposed to have been Chris who died that day. He had been the target.

All these years she'd blamed Chris, so sure her brother couldn't have made a mistake. She had been right. He hadn't made a mistake, but then, neither had Chris.

Both of them were blameless. She had wronged Chris. And her mother and father had also wronged him. But they couldn't make amends. That burden fell completely on Sia's shoulders.

Anger she'd never felt before infused her with a searing heat. Without a word, she left the stateroom. She could hear Chris calling her name, but she was too caught up in the emotion to stop, to reason, to give a damn about anything. When she reached the legal office, she burst into the cabin.

Susan Cotes jumped in her seat as the door slammed against the wall. She reacted visibly to the look in Sia's eyes. She rose and started to back up. Without preamble, Sia lunged at the woman, grabbed her by the shirtfront and pushed her into the bulkhead. "You ruined my life. You killed my brother."

Susan Cotes's eyes filled with confusion and fear. She shook her head. "I don't know what you're talking about."

Strong hands grabbed at Sia and pulled her off and away from Susan. Chris stepped forward and said softly, "Get ahold of yourself."

Sia shouted, "You're a monster."

Susan looked at Chris and said, "What is she saying? Why is she so upset? I don't even know her brother."

Chris pulled out his handcuffs and Susan's eyes widened, tears gathered. "No," she said her voice breaking. "I didn't do anything. I didn't kill anyone."

"Susan Cotes, you're under arrest for the murder of Lieutenant Eli Washington."

He turned her around and snapped the cuffs on her wrists. Susan shouted, "This is crazy. I didn't kill him!"

Chris ignored her words and said, "You have the right to remain silent…"

His words faded as she stared at the woman responsible for so many deaths. What sick, twisted mind could have planned eight murders? But she had killed nine men! And only Chris had survived. Guilt rolled and tumbled around in her gut as she looked at him staying calm and doing his duty. She watched mutely as he turned the woman over to the masters-at-arms with instructions to put her in the brig.

Sia turned away from the door, crossing her arms over her chest and trying to tamp down her anger.

When the door closed behind them, Chris turned to her. "Sia, what were you thinking! You have no proof she's done anything but kill Washington."

She turned to meet his eyes, but dropped her gaze down at the way he looked at her, disappointment clear in them. She unwrapped her arms. He continued.

His voice was closer, which meant so was he. She had to look up, but she really needed more space, and more time, before having to handle him, or handle anything. Dealing with Chris up close in her personal space was more than she could take on at the moment. "You're a seasoned prosecutor, and you had better start thinking like one."

"It has to be her," Sia said stubbornly. "Did you see the photos? Did you? They all look like you! Oh, God, you were a victim. She was trying to kill you and yet she stands there looking so innocent."

"You need to step away from Rafael's death. You're

letting your grief and anger get in the way of rational thought. You need to get back on track right now or I'm taking you off this case!"

"You will not!"

His eyes went hard and flinty, and she had to resist the urge to shiver. "I will and I have the authority." Gone were the smooth-as-velvet, dulcet tones. In their place was a flat, steely voice that brooked no argument.

He took a step closer, and she tensed. She tried not to show it, but that much was really beyond her at the moment. The stabilized world she'd thought she'd constructed for herself had just been proven to have very shaky foundations. And she didn't know what to do about that. All these years, she'd gone on the assumption that Chris was at fault, not forgiving him, not allowing herself to pine for him. She had wanted him so badly, for the comfort, for the peace, but she couldn't find it with him. And now she realized, she hadn't found it without him either. She felt adrift and lost.

"We have a lot of work to do. Foremost being looking into those other deaths and getting the details. We will need to be calm and prepared when we talk to her again. You can't come barreling in here and accuse her of a murder where we have no proof. Get ahold of yourself, now!"

The conflagration of her anger dissipated, leaving a small, burning ember inside her. He was right. She had lost it. After so many years of grief and loss filling her up, she'd snapped. Her bottled-up feelings had broken free and if not for Chris, she could have jeopardized this solid case against Susan Cotes. It was a good thing he was here.

She took a cleansing breath and headed for the door. When Chris didn't move, she tossed him a chiding look. "Aren't you coming?"

"Where?" he said, eyeing her warily.

"To the captain. We have to search her bunk."

He nodded and opened the door, "Now you're talking. After you."

Sia donned gloves after they entered Susan's berth, the one she shared with Lieutenant Maria Jackson. Sia started with her locker and Chris worked on searching the bunk.

Without thinking about it, she went straight for the socks and began pulling them apart. After the forth pair a familiar bottle dropped out. Sia looked down, her stomach twisting. Bending down, she picked up the bottle and gasped.

"What is it?" Chris asked.

"This is the exact same bottle I found in the master chief's berth. What appears to be a simple over-the-counter irregularity aid."

"How do you know that?"

"The label was torn in the exact same spot. You find anything?"

"Yes and no. I found her yellow tunic stuffed under her mattress. I bagged it to test for gun residue. But no gun."

"One more question to ask her."

"Let's get this cataloged as evidence and get it to Math. He's still at Hickam. In the meantime, we need to slog through the information your aide sent us regarding those deaths. Let's get to it."

"Yes, sir," Sia said.

After getting the sample off to Math, they returned to her cabin for her laptop, went to the legal office and printed out all the information her aide had sent her. They decided that it would be more comfortable working out of her own stateroom and returned there.

If they were going to tie these murders to Susan Cotes, there was a lot to go over. She was also still waiting on the information regarding the master chief.

"What was her connection to the master chief?"

"He was sleeping with her?"

"He was old enough to be her father."

"Maybe she's looking for a father figure. All we know at this point is he tried to protect her. I think that's why he tried to kill you."

"It's possible. I told him I was going to dig into my brother's death. That could have been the trigger."

"You couldn't have known he was connected at the time, Sia."

"Yes, well, I almost signed my own death warrant." She looked down at his notebook. "You've got a lot of notes there. Care to share?"

"All nine pilot murders involve pilots stationed aboard the *McCloud*," Chris said.

Sia was surprised no one had put the pattern together, but more than one agent had handled the deaths.

"The first death resulted from a fall from an upper deck of the carrier. It had been windy and storming and the death was ruled accidental. One was during shore leave. The man had been stabbed and left for dead outside a bar in Hawaii. NCIS investigated and classified it as a robbery/homicide. No suspect had ever been found in that crime and it's now considered a cold case." He flipped over a page and continued. "The next was a chopper pilot who had crashed into the ocean and drowned. The ruling had been accidental."

Sia wondered if the pilot had been drugged.

"Then your brother was killed, ruled pilot error. Two more pilots had gone down on a routine mission, but their jets and bodies hadn't ever been recovered."

"Then that left Saunders and Washington," she said, looking over his shoulder.

"Your aide is very thorough."

"That he is. He'll make a very good lawyer one day."

Chris's phone trilled, he flipped it open and said, "It's a text from Math. Get him up on the two-way."

When Math popped up on the screen, he said, "You two look as tired as I feel."

"What do you have for us?" Sia asked.

"For you, sweetheart, anything you want." He wagged his eyebrows.

"Math," Chris growled.

"Oh, right, you have a claim on her."

"Shut up and give us the information."

"Which is it, man? Shut up or talk?"

"Math," Chris said, lower and more menacing.

"All right. The drug in the bottle is Gamma-Hydroxybutyric acid, commonly known as GHB."

"The date-rape drug?" Sia asked.

"Yes. GHB is also used in a medical setting as a general anesthetic, to treat conditions such as insomnia, clinical depression, narcolepsy and alcoholism, as well as to improve athletic performance."

"But it wasn't prescribed for her. It was in an over-the-counter medication bottle."

"That's correct. We can surmise from that behavior she meant to conceal the drug. So if we can infer that, then we can conclude she used it to drug Washington. It would explain his behavior the night he crashed and his inability to eject."

"But there was no evidence Washington had been drugged."

"GHB is colorless and odorless and is easily added to drinks that mask the flavor. A urine test is the best way to detect the drug in the system, and that is problematic, if you're not specifically looking for it. The drug leaves the body about eight to twelve hours after ingestion. Quite frankly, the ME could have missed it, since it is sodium-based and occurs naturally in the central nervous system."

"Is there a way to detect it after death if you're specifically looking for it?"

Math smiled. "You would have made a good forensic scientist, Vargas. As a matter of fact, there is. GHB can be detected in hair for months after ingesting the drug."

"And you already tested Lieutenant Washington's hair?" Chris's smile was easy and made her shiver inside as she became mesmerized by the way his mouth curved.

"I did. He had enough in his system to cause dizziness and drowsiness. I would say if Lieutenant Washington and your suspect were in the wardroom, she could have easily slipped it into his drink. Since he had coffee in his stomach contents, the strong flavor would have easily masked the taste."

"And the tunic?"

"Well, you've really hit the jackpot with this woman. The tunic tested positive for gunpowder residue. She had fired a weapon, but I can't say for certain if it was at you and the lovely Sia or at the pistol range. If you want me to do any tests on the other pilots who were killed, you'll have to exhume the bodies. That's always hell on the families," Math said, shaking his head.

"It may be necessary. Their loved ones have a right to know what really happened to them," Chris said firmly.

"You let me know, cowboy."

"Roger that. Math, thanks as always. I appreciate the effort you made coming all the way from Norfolk."

"Can I go home now?"

"Yes…after I get your reports."

"Aw, damn, that'll take me hours. Looks like I'll have to sleep on the plane."

"Well, you better get started."

"Screw you, Vargas," Math said with a chuckle. "Goodbye, pretty Sia." He blew her a kiss and ended the conversation as the screen winked out.

"He's a character," she said.

"You have no idea. He's brilliant, but eccentric. He loves the ladies."

She smiled. "I can tell." Her eyes locked with his. In this quiet moment, a moment of shared amusement, it was hard to think that six years had passed since she'd seen Chris. It was as if time hadn't passed at all. As if they were in some kind of time warp transporting them back to when her life was full of this man, his kisses, his body, his love.

She couldn't forget the past, but right now it seemed to recede some, to give her some solace in this moment.

Strands of hair slipped from her bun and swung softly against her cheek.

Chris reached out and brushed at it, letting the long strands filter through his fingers. Her hair was free from the bun by some stealth move he made and as it cascaded over her shoulders, Chris sighed. "My beautiful Sia."

Nerve endings on red alert, Sia held his heavy-lidded gaze, his eyes as gray as smoke. It seemed amazing to her, the way her body came alive and aware of him. Her heart picked up a beat; her breasts grew heavy and tingled, her nipples drawing into hard, beaded knots.

Chris was tall and rangy, with strong broad shoulders and slim hips. Sleek skin over heavy muscle. The expression on his lean, tanned face was languid and powerful. He moved closer to her as his hand cupped her face. As he looked deep into her eyes, she remembered easily why she had fallen for Chris so quickly.

He'd been cocky and brash when she'd first met him. Imbued with that fighter pilot aura only a man with deep confidence and amazing skill could have and, damn, but he looked good in the uniform. He was first in his class at Top Gun and she hadn't at first wanted to get involved with him. She had plans and he didn't fit into them. But then she'd seen his sensitive side, when he would coax her mother out of her depressions and make her father laugh with his big whopping fighter pilot stories.

His moniker had been Streak, like lightning, like pure unadulterated speed. And he liked to move fast.

Like a flash, he had taken her breath away.

Moving fast had been in his blood, but it looked like he'd tempered that speed until only the promise of it lay in his dark, soot-smudged eyes.

He caught her first with the magnetic quality of those eyes, glittering with devilish lights, and then zapped her with that grin. She had never experienced anything like Chris Vargas's grin. She felt as if he had turned a thousand watts of pure electricity on her.

His mouth was wide, his lips were sculpted, the sexy dip in his upper lip drew her eye and all she could think about was how he would taste.

He went to his knees on the bunk and cupped her face in both of his hands. His palms were warm against her skin and she closed her eyes as he ran his thumbs along her cheekbones. With a quick intake of air, he whispered close to her ear, "You trying to seduce me, sugar?"

She shivered at his warm breath across the sensitive shell of her ear. His fingers delved into her hair, caressing the nape of her neck.

"Why don't you take your shirt off for me?"

She complied, but not before she slid her hands up his sides, up to the heavy muscles of his shoulders. Her buttons felt small compared to all that strength.

Her shirt off and discarded, Sia opened her eyes. The scent of him filled her nostrils with warm, aroused male, musky and virile.

That mobile mouth skimmed along her face with teasing kisses; the whisper of his heated lips almost made her beg for more contact. "Now the pants," he ordered. And Sia knew, in this case, she was at his command.

She shifted and he shifted with her as if he couldn't bear to let her go. She slipped out of her pants and knelt on the bunk in nothing but her bra and panties.

"Soldier on the outside…" he said as he deftly removed her bra and released her breasts; they ached for his touch. He hooked his fingers around the stretch of lace at her hip, his flesh hot against her skin. "All woman on the inside."

He tugged. Slowly. Excruciatingly slowly. She wanted to tip her head back, close her eyes, and just focus on feeling every sensation, every ripple of pleasure. But she couldn't take her eyes off him. She tried not to tremble so hard, but she couldn't seem to stop. As he removed her panties, the warm cotton of his pullover barely brushing over her nipples, she cried out.

"Sia," he said, his voice strangled. "You're so beautiful."

She watched as he stood and quickly undressed and donned protection. "Lean back and open your knees slightly," he said, crawling back on the bunk. Sia complied, meeting his eyes in a head-on collision of passion.

He knelt before her again. This time his hands circled her waist and slid to her lower back. He put slight pressure there and she helplessly arched. He supported her back as his head descended to lick like flame against her collarbone. A puff of air blown across her nipple was a tease, sending red-hot ripples straight to her groin.

He licked one nipple, then the other and Sia groaned softly in her throat, aching for more contact with his hot, wet mouth.

She reached for him, sliding her hands over his taut, smooth skin, into the silk of his hair. With pressure on the back of his head, she brought his mouth hard against her breast. His mouth closed over it, working the beaded point with his tongue, his five-o'clock shadow pleasantly abrading her skin.

With urging, he clamped his lips over her other breast, suckling her until she thought the pleasure might kill her.

He slipped a hand between her thighs to find the tight, throbbing knot of nerves. Gently he pushed her back, his mouth still on her breast. When she was flat on her back, he slipped away from her, trailing kisses down her abdomen. As he slowly drew his tongue along her most sensitive flesh, Sia restlessly moved against him. Chris moaned as he continued his dedicated assault on her senses, tying her into sensuous knots. He slipped his fingers inside of her, his tongue never stopping its delicious swirling patterns that stole her breath. She buried her hands in his hair, gripping it gently as long moans, one after the other, poured out of her as he lifted her and settled his mouth fully against her.

Crying out, her mind reeling at the pleasure, at the pure carnal joy. Her hips arched and bucked, twisted for the best angle and optimum contact with his mouth.

Hot, wild bliss. Mindless ecstasy. Terrifying freedom from the bounds she had to live within. Her pleasure crested abruptly, strongly, wringing unrestrained cries from her.

Pleasure spiraled through her and she was in his arms, immersed in his embrace, lost in his kiss as that beautiful mouth covered hers. His touch unleashed a host of needs that had lain dormant inside of her for six long, lonely years. Now they leaped and twisted, wild with the prospect of freedom.

As their eyes met, she saw his glittering on the edge of control. He entered her in one powerful stroke, filling her, touching off another explosive climax that only fueled him. He wrapped his arms around her and crushed her to him.

He moved slowly and she could tell by his taut muscles it cost him. He kissed her softly, tenderly.

She slid her hands down his back, over the hot, flexing, sweat-slick muscles. Then her fingers stretched over the tight, rounded mounds of his buttocks. She caressed and squeezed, urging him to increase his tempo until he was pumping his hips into her, frantic with the need for release they achieved, one on the heels of the other.

Afterward they dozed, exhausted, replete. Chris settled on his side with one leg thrown across Sia. She turned toward him and curled up against him as his arms came around her and pulled her closer. She caressed his face, the sharp cheekbones, ran her thumb across his mouth, loving the texture of his skin.

Inside she felt a heaviness settle on her as she met his eyes. There was no satisfaction in them, no triumph, just a deep sadness that connected with her own heavy heart.

Her brain scrambled to make sense out of the constant flux with the reaction of her body and her heart. It was all such a huge jumble. There was no way she could make a rational judgment. Not with him looking at her like that, and her wanting all sorts of things that were on the verge of impossible.

Their past still loomed, and with this new information that still had her reeling, she lost her anchor. Then he cupped her cheek and turned her gaze to his when she looked away in a vain effort to regroup.

"Does it help to know?" he whispered in the dark stateroom.

"Know what?"

"Who might have been responsible for the death of your brother. She used me like a weapon and killed the wrong man. Does it help?" he asked, never more sincere, real concern outlined in every inch of his handsome face.

This time her heart didn't skip; it stopped altogether, then thundered on with such ferocity she felt it might explode from the sudden intensity of it.

"Don't," she said softly, her voice catching. She buried her face in his neck. "Just hold me, Chris. Tighter," she said. "As if you'll never let me go."

"I remember, Sia. All the time. I remember what it was like to be with you, hold you. I thought I had gotten over you, but it seems that I was wrong. I don't know what we're accomplishing with this trip down memory lane, but I can't say that I wouldn't do it again. I've missed you, sweetheart."

Guilt and shame welled up in her that he could be so generous and she was unable to get past what had happened. There were going to be more questions for Susan Cotes. But would there be any answers for Sia?

"Talk to me. Tell me what is in your heart. It's just a matter of saying the words. I won't pressure you after this. Just tell me. Does it make a difference?"

This was killing her, twisting her heart and emotions into painful, complicated knots. Did she still love Chris? Did finding out Rafael's death had been a result of an attempt on Chris's life help? Could she turn away from a once-in-a-lifetime relationship again?

"I don't know, Chris." Her voice broke and she buried her face in his neck, her hot tears spilling out against his smooth skin. He tightened his hold, which only made her cry harder. She didn't deserve his comfort, trapped in her own bitterness and pain.

In that moment, she realized with such clarity how she had betrayed him, abandoned him. Even now, she couldn't come to terms with her own actions. It was easier to continue to blame him, take what little time they had together, then part when it was over.

"I simply just don't know."

Chapter 10

Dawn was breaking across a tumble of heavy gray clouds. Sia tucked her hands in her coat pockets and made her way toward the bridge followed closely by the master-at-arms she'd requested to accompany her. The wind picked up and snatched at her tightly pinned hair beneath her hat.

She was still trying to make sense of everything that had happened in the last day. But she still had a job to do. When she reached the bridge, she removed her cover and found the captain drinking a cup of coffee as he surveyed information on a clipboard.

"Good morning, Lieutenant. I'm afraid we have some rough seas ahead of us. There's a storm between us and the coast. No way to go around it. We're going to push to land. I'm going to clear the flight deck and restrict all crew to their quarters. Are you aware of safety procedures in the case of an emergency?"

"Yes, Billy—Commander Stryker went over them with me after I boarded. I'm up to speed."

He nodded. "Good work on getting Washington's killer."

"About that, sir." She pulled out the sheaf of papers she'd brought with her. "We suspect there are more." She handed him the pages and he shuffled through them, staring at the pictures of all the dead pilots and their resemblance to each other.

"Son of a bitch," he said softly.

"We, Special Agent Vargas and I, believe all these men were her victims. But at this point we don't have any proof."

"What do you plan to do?"

"Get a confession. We think the killer has some deep-seated issues regarding pilots. The first guy was probably pushed to his death. He was either lured to the deck or was a case of opportunity."

"You have my permission to do whatever it takes to get the confession. You're a lawyer. I don't have to remind you of the law."

"Sir, there's something else. Something I didn't mention when I boarded because I didn't know it was part of this investigation."

"Go on."

"Special Agent Vargas and I know each other. We had a relationship six years ago when he was stationed aboard the *McCloud*. He was involved in a midair crash that killed my brother, Rafael Soto. We believe he was the intended target of the killer and my brother died as a result of the attempt on his life."

"I was briefed on the incident when I took control of

this vessel five years ago. I sense you have an agenda here, Commander. Perhaps you should tell me what it is."

"Sir, I never meant to harbor any secrets. Until this evidence came to light, I always believed it had been an accident. I also believed my brother was blameless in the matter. But now, with this new evidence, I was hoping you would recommend to SECNAV that my brother's case get a review so he has a chance to be cleared of the pilot-error ruling. I want to petition to have him memorialzed at the Navy Memorial."

"You get me a confession and I'll petition to clear both their names."

"I don't know how Chris feels about it, sir."

"You didn't consult him?"

"No, our relationship has been strained. I didn't want to presume too much on his behalf, but I will relay your promise to him."

Sia turned to leave. When she reached the door, the captain said, "I'm sorry for your loss, Commander. You're a fine credit to this Navy. Your brother would have been proud."

"Thank you, sir."

When she got to the base of the ladder, she could see the bustle of the crew working to get the deck cleared and the jets stowed below in the hangar. As she turned to go inside and head back to her quarters, she spied Chris standing on the deck. He looked forlorn and alone as the wind caught in his dark hair. His face was impassive as he confronted his ghosts and she had no doubt that's exactly what he was doing. She watched as he clenched trembling hands.

Her heart ached for him. He was part of the past she wanted to forget, part of the bitterness and the grief and the pain.

Chris stood on the windblown deck trying to rein in his emotions. Trying to come to grips with his own loss. *It had been more, Rafe,* he said. *I lost more than you that day. I lost Sia. I lost a family and I lost my nerve. But I've got to finally, finally come to terms with it.*

Once he had known dreams of love and family and the kind of ordinary success that most men strove for, but he'd been shown in no uncertain terms that life had a way of taking you and tossing you around like a rag doll to lie broken where you fell. That life had blown up in his face, and he had had to live with the fact he'd been the one to lay the powder and light the fuse, or so he had thought.

What he had rebuilt for himself in the aftermath was simple and basic, he reminded himself as he watched the last jet sink onto the deck of the carrier; the sound of the hydraulic platforms descending into the belly of the deck was snatched away by the wind.

As it disappeared, he let his pain go with it, let his guilt and his shame disappear. He clenched his hands into fists as he struggled with the hope that one day Sia could do the same. He didn't want simple and basic anymore. He wanted the *more* he had lost.

With the thought of her, he felt her small hand curl around his fist. He opened his hand and grasped hers. The warmth was welcome as it radiated from his hand to his empty heart.

"There's a storm brewing. The captain is restricting crew to quarters for the duration."

"That include us?"

"Yes, but in light of this new information regarding the GHB, I want to reinterview Lieutenant Russell and Monroe. If we can place Susan in the wardroom at the same time as both pilots, that gives us stronger evidence that she had the opportunity to spike both of their drinks. I also have the captain's permission to work on Susan Cotes and get her to confess. We have the information to present to her. I also asked for my brother's case to be reopened and considered."

He turned to her. "Don't you think that was premature? We don't have a confession yet. We don't have anything that links her to that accident."

"We will. We have to. The captain said he would also petition to clear your name."

"I don't need my name cleared. It doesn't matter anymore. The past is over and done with. I'm moving on."

"Surely you can't mean that. What you did with the Navy means something. It has to. If it doesn't, then my brother's death means nothing. I can't bear that."

He turned to her and pulled her close. "I didn't say that what I did here didn't mean anything, Sia."

She wrapped her arms around his neck. "I wish it was as easy for me to let go," she said.

"But you can't."

"Not yet. Maybe never. I don't know."

She grasped his hand and pulled him toward the decks below. They went to her quarters and when the door shut behind them, they didn't pretend.

His mouth found hers with evidence of a keen-edged

need that was reciprocated. This time would be different from last night. He wanted to unleash the need he had for her that lurked just beneath the surface.

The air crackled with the electricity they created. His mouth went in search of hers, and their tongues tangled. He pushed at her clothing until he got it all off her, and she did the same.

He bent his head to catch her nipple in his lips and sucked strongly from her. Her knees buckled in sudden violent response. Her fingers went to his hair, unconsciously drawing him closer as the sensations crashed over him, one wave after another.

She cupped his heavy shaft and he surged into her soft hand. It was shockingly arousing to be touched by her and he knew he would never get enough. He slipped his hand between their bodies, found her warm, wet heat and stroked a finger inside her. She cried out, her fingers tightening around him. His mouth went to her other breast in a dual assault that was engineered to make her unravel fast.

His voice was ragged, muffled against her skin. "The bunk."

Her touch grew more deliberate. "I want you inside me. Now."

His breathing ragged, he gave her a long, deep kiss, and began to move her toward the bunk. She apparently had no intention of cooperating. "The bunk," he panted, his mouth moving to her jaw, her ear, her throat. "Now, Sia."

Instead she went to her knees before him, pressed her lips against his hardness. He shuddered and groaned, throwing his head back at the feel of her soft mouth taking him. She traced her tongue down the length of him, exploring him with lips and tongue, until he hauled her to her feet and into his arms.

Her mouth met his fiercely. Her kiss evoked a violent response in him. He responded to her violence with more of the same, demanding an answer. He backed her against the bulkhead, then reached down and lifted her leg over his hip.

The need in her clear brown eyes aroused him beyond his limits. "Chris." He pressed his mouth to hers and swallowed the sound while cupping her bottom and lifting her to impale her with one long stroke.

The sweet velvet slide of his shaft inside her, the delicate pulsations as her body adjusted to his invasion, was almost more than he could bear.

Surging forward, he heard her moan and went in search of her mouth. Sealing it with his, he positioned his hips, thrusting hard and deep, wringing wild cries from her. Her legs were wrapped around him, her arms clinging to his shoulders. Each savage thrust flattened her breasts against him and the exquisite sensations threatened to send him over the edge.

Fingers digging into her bottom, he held her steady as he pounded into her, his vision graying, beginning to blur. He dimly felt her heels pressing into his back, her body tensing, then clenching around him. He was blind, deaf to all but this woman.

When he felt her release, he lunged harder, buried himself inside her to the hilt and followed her into oblivion.

They made it, eventually, to the bunk. For a few minutes they lay there. Once their breathing softened and slowed, Sia turned to him. "You look like you came to some kind of closure up there on the flight deck."

"Almost. I only need one more thing."

"What is that?"

"You to say that you forgive me, Sia. Say the words."

"Give me some more time, Chris. Just a little bit more."

He sighed in disappointment, but Sia couldn't seem to utter the words. She didn't know why. She should. Chris really didn't deserve this.

She had no idea what time it was when her eyes flew open. Nor could she say what had woken her from such a deep sleep. She went to move, then felt the weight of Chris's arm folded across her back, holding her against him. She didn't want to disturb him, but she was struggling to orient herself and her still-fuzzy brain took a moment or two to remember where she was and what she was doing there.

With the sudden dipping and rolling of the carrier, Sia felt a dull throb of a headache beginning as she lifted her head, willing her eyes to adjust to the dark so she could find her bedside clock. It was just past 0930, which was a relief. She had only been asleep for about an hour. It seemed neither one of them had gotten a decent night's sleep.

Of course, Navy bunks weren't exactly meant to be shared by two, yet she felt completely and blissfully sated. She thought about that for a moment, partly because it pushed the return of fear and panic to the edges of her mind for a few more precious seconds, and partly because she couldn't help but wonder what, in fact, did come next for them. She realized the events currently unfolding could end up robbing her of finding out, but that didn't stop her from thinking about what she'd want if it was up to her.

Slowly, cautiously, she slipped out from beneath his arm and gently shifted her weight off the bunk, her eyes adjusting just enough to keep her from stumbling on her way to her toiletry items.

She hit the shower and the heated water felt good even with the unsteady deck rolling beneath her feet. She was supremely proud her stomach didn't protest. Seasickness would be absolutely no fun.

Her father would have been proud of her, she thought as she exited the head and slipped back inside the stateroom. The thought made her smile and for the first time since he'd died, she was thankful she was able to think of him without the immediate pain that would inevitably follow.

She snapped on a light near the locker. It was enough to illuminate her clothing and she dressed quickly in her service khaki. After she was dressed, she walked over to Chris, who was still sleeping. She noted the smudges under his eyes. They deserved this small bit of rest. He had kept long hours on this case, not to mention the extra pain and baggage each of them carried.

Now was the time to get the confession from the woman who was directly responsible for her brother's death. It was what she hoped for so that she could finally lay him to rest.

Proof, evidence. Her brain hammered on the words, and she paced away from the bunk. Even with Susan Cotes's confession, was there a chance for them?

She suspected that it was up to her.

"You're going to wear a hole in the deck."

Her head whipped to the bunk. Chris was awake, his sleepy half-lidded eyes watching her. His head was propped on his arm, his biceps a thick bulge of muscle. His shoulders gleamed in the dim light and cast shadows on his broad chest and tapered waist.

"I was just thinking about our upcoming session with Susan Cotes."

"Working out a strategy?" he asked, stretching his tall, muscular body like a big jungle cat.

"Something like that," she replied, her brain short-circuiting at the sight of him.

He smiled. "You must be a hellcat in court."

She shook off her fascination and turned away to look for her hat. "If you mean that I get my convictions or garner a good defense, then yes, I'm a hellcat in court."

"Come here."

His voice was thick and velvety and she'd be a fool to even get near him in this mood.

"Chris," she said, her eyes going over his face again, homing in on his mouth. "That's not a good idea. I just got dressed and pinned up my hair. I'm not going to get close enough for that stealth move you do to bring it all back down again."

He laughed. "Stealth move?"

"That's what I call it."

"I can't entice you even a little?" He wagged his eyebrows.

She laughed, but kept herself at a safe distance from him. "It's tempting."

"I guess I'll have to come to you." He slipped out of the bunk, all heavy muscle and testosterone, his maleness emphasized by his wide chest and thick thighs.

She couldn't take her eyes off him. Rooted to the spot, she was helpless when he reached her and cupped her cheek. His mouth covered hers, the kiss full of banked passion and subtle need.

When he raised his head, he smiled. "I'll use your shower, then make a quick trip to my stateroom for clothes."

It wasn't until a full minute after he stepped into her bathroom that she realized her hair was down around her shoulders. With an exasperated, but amused sigh, she went to pin it up again.

Looking at herself in the mirror, she couldn't quite meet her own eyes. Maybe she couldn't say it to him now, but she could—had to—admit it to herself. She was still in love with him, and it solved absolutely nothing.

Fifteen minutes later she was sitting next to Chris, trying not to get distracted by the fresh way he smelled and the heat that radiated off his body, a body she had just done such intimate things with less than an hour ago.

Lieutenant Russell, Saunders's wingman, sat in front of her. She smiled at him and said, "Can you remember who was in the wardroom the day of Saunders's crash?"

Lieutenant Russell looked down as he fidgeted with his hat. "There were a couple of other pilots there, Green and Wilson. Also, I remember the LSO, Maria

Jackson, was getting coffee and Lieutenant Cotes was there talking to Lieutenant Jackson."

Sia nodded her head. "Thank you, Lieutenant. You've been a great help."

After he left, Lieutenant Monroe was ushered in and he recalled that both Lieutenant Jackson and Cotes were in the wardroom. Lieutenant Cotes and Washington were sniping at each other and giving each other dirty looks. This evidence was the last nail in Susan's coffin.

Focus, she told herself as the master-at-arms opened the door and ushered Susan Cotes in. Chris indicated for her to sit at the small table and, with an irritated sigh, she sat down.

"Do you understand the charges against you?"

"I understand them, but you're both off base. I didn't kill Lieutenant Washington. I don't know how many times I have to say it."

"The evidence makes you a liar, Lieutenant."

Susan's face blanched and she brought her hands up, the metal cuffs rattling against the table. "What evidence?" she demanded, fear and defiance in her tone.

"We found your fingerprints on the radar casing from his jet. The one you tampered with, along with the GHB you used to drug him."

Susan stood in outrage, her face a mask of shock and disbelief. "I did not! I had nothing to do with it."

"The evidence is iron-clad, Lieutenant. We didn't bring you here so you could deny your guilt. That's unproductive in the face of the evidence. Both lieutenant Russell and Monroe place you in the wardroom before each pilot took off."

It surprised Sia that Susan was fighting tears and

she suddenly became uncomfortable. Susan's behavior seemed wrong, somehow. She showed no signs of the sadistic behavior of a serial killer. But the evidence was irrefutable and Sia put away her doubts.

"Why did you bring me here?"

"We want to give you a chance to come clean about the other murders."

"Other murders? Oh, my God. You two are insane. I haven't committed *any* murders."

Without speaking, Sia laid out the pictures of the dead pilots. Susan looked down at them with a dull and glassy-eyed stare. "I don't know any of these men."

"We think you do." Sia pointed out her brother. "This is the only man in this array who doesn't resemble the others. Do you know why?"

"No," Susan mumbled and Sia could tell when someone was shutting down.

"It's because he was an unintended victim. Chris was your intended target."

Susan looked at Chris, then back at Sia, then down to the picture. "This is your brother, isn't it?"

"That's right."

She looked at Chris. "He was killed when your plane crashed into his. I remember that report."

Chris nodded.

"Wait a second," Sia said as she digested Susan's words. "Report?"

"That's right, Commander," she said smugly. "I wasn't on the *McCloud* when Lieutenant Soto died. I was thousands of miles away in Virginia, at Norfolk Naval Airbase at a training center."

* * *

Sia looked at the computer screen in her quarters, dejected by the news her legalman gave her. "It's true, Commander. She had orders and it's documented on her record. She wasn't on the *McCloud* the day your brother was killed. I'm sorry." The picture was fuzzy and jumped often as the storm battered the ship.

She tried hard to hide her disappointment. "And the other pilots?"

"Those dates match up to her tour of duty. Her shore leave matches up to the time our dead pilot ended up in that alley."

"Thank you, McBride."

"You're welcome, Commander. When are you headed home?"

"As soon as we dock. We'll process Cotes and Chris and I will hop a plane back to Norfolk. She's going to be handled by the folks in Miramar."

"It's getting hard to hear you. How is it there?"

"The storm is pretty intense, but the captain is competent."

"Good. Oh, I almost forgot. I finished compiling the list of all the personnel aboard the *McCloud* the day your brother died. I can send that to you."

"Please do."

There was a knock at the door and Sia signed off on the two-way.

When she opened it, Chris stood on the other side. "How are you doing?"

"I'm angry and disappointed. How do you think I feel?" She moved away from him, afraid he would try to soothe her. She didn't want that.

"That would be my guess. I warned you not to get your hopes up too high," Chris said.

"Yes, you did, and now that you've delivered your message, you can go," Sia snapped.

"Sia, what is it you're looking for?" Chris began on a long, bone-weary sigh. "What do you need?"

"I want my brother's life to have had meaning. The Navy Memorial is something tangible. Something that people will remember. Oh, never mind. You don't understand."

His big shoulders rose, absorbing the weight of the accusation. "Yes, I do. I understand too well. Do you think that blaming someone, anyone, will somehow give your brother's death meaning?"

"Yes!" she said, slamming the heel of her hand against the bulkhead. "It wasn't his fault he died. He's not to blame."

"No, he's not. I am. There's no hiding it now. There's nobody out there left to blame but me. You can't give me the forgiveness I need because you need to hold on to that blame. It's ruled your life for so long you can't seem to let it go."

"Leave me alone." He was right and she didn't want to hear it. She couldn't let go until she'd attained her goal. She couldn't let her brother down as she had somehow let her parents down.

"Maybe you don't want to let go," Chris said relentlessly, grabbing her shoulders so she would look into his face, into his eyes.

"Leave," she shouted, her lips trembling, her anger getting the best of her. "Now!" She struggled out of his grasp, her eyes on fire and her throat full.

He turned toward the door. "Maybe it would have been easier for you if I had died that day, too. Maybe then you could have moved on."

She didn't answer him. She couldn't. In her disappointment and grief, she was unable to make any sense out of what had happened. And she could get no justice for her brother or for Chris. But she did know one single truth about this whole business. Her world would have been so bleak if Chris had died. The thought of being in a world without him caused her more pain than she could bear.

The door closed behind him and she knew if there had ever been a chance, there no longer was. She'd ruined it by being unable to make that simple concession.

She heard her email ding. It looked as if Gabriel had stayed overtime to get her what she needed. She was sorry she wasted his time. They had their killer and Susan couldn't have been the person who had tried to kill Chris. It was baffling. Sia had been so sure. *All* the other men looked like him, to the point of eeriness.

Unless Susan was telling the truth and she hadn't killed Lieutenant Washington. Did they have the wrong woman? The thought left her feeling dizzy and weak. She stood there for a moment pushing all her pain and disappointment away.

The fingerprints were damning evidence, though. *The fingerprints were perfect.* Perfect...maybe. Sia sat down at her computer and pulled up the internet browser. She typed in "faking fingerprints." Numerous hits came up and she chose a website. It was possible and, furthermore, the fingerprints that were faked were usually flawless.

She quickly pulled up the file of personnel and started to go through the list. She found the master chief's name, and Susan Cotes's. She scanned the list until her breath caught and her senses heightened. The only other familiar name on the list was still aboard the ship. With trembling hands she pulled up the person's file. Not only had the person been on the ship at the time of all the deaths, but that person had also been on the ship at the time of Rafael's death.

A knock sounded on the door and Sia rose to answer, still intent on her discovery. Chris had come back. She should have known he couldn't leave her alone in her state, and she was grateful to him. The ship pitched violently, and Sia held on to the doorjamb before she reached for the knob.

An apology was on her lips when she pulled the door open. But the eyes she met weren't Chris's.

Lieutenant Maria Jackson. She was the only other person who had been on the ship when the murders occurred. In her eyes was the coldness Sia had expected from Susan Cotes.

The eyes of a serial killer.

Chapter 11

"Hello, Sia. Surprised to see me?"

"Lieutenant Jackson." It was all she could get out, because she'd looked past her face now and discovered the gun in her hand.

She gestured with it now. "The Navy JAG got caught off guard. That's so delicious."

Sia couldn't move, couldn't think clearly, couldn't decide on any course of action, because too many things were racing through her brain all at once. Susan Cotes was telling the truth. She was innocent. Would she ever get the chance to tell Chris she was sorry, that she still loved him?

"Move back inside."

She hesitated, not wanting to comply, debating for a split second whether to step back, slam the door shut.

"The bullet is faster than your reflexes, Commander," she said calmly, as if reading her mind. "It's not the way I want it to happen, but…" She shrugged. Once again she gestured for Sia to back up. "You have questions and I have answers. Do you want to go to your death not knowing what those answers are?"

Sia stepped back as Maria shoved her hard into the stateroom and closed the door.

She pointed at the locker. "Change."

Sia's gaze flew to the locker. "Into what?"

"Your dress blues."

"Why?"

"Indulge me and I'll allow you one question."

Sia walked over to the locker and pulled out her uniform. As she took off her shirt she asked, "Did you try to kill Chris six years ago by spiking his coffee with GHB and tampering with his radar?"

"Yes."

"Why?"

"That's two questions."

Sia seethed as she ripped off her shirt and donned the white one, then stopped.

"Aw, the JAG officer wants to play games."

"Answer the question."

"I did you a favor. Men are nothing but abusers and leavers. You can't trust them. I will admit there was a lot of satisfaction killing them inside their fighters. Cocky bastards. But it was even more satisfying up close when they knew they were going to die. You should have seen the look on the face of the one I pushed off the deck. And the one I stabbed to death. So surprised a woman would ever want to do anything more than fawn over him. They made me sick."

Sia listened, shocked and repulsed at the lack of feel-

ing in her voice. She was completely devoid of con-
science. Emotionless, soulless. There would be no
appealing to her sense of mercy or humanity, because
she didn't have any. Escape was her only hope, and that
hope was slim with the gun pointed at her back.

"Chris isn't like that."

Her expression changed. "No, he isn't. He was loyal
to you and kind. I will give you that. But he looked like
him and that made it okay to kill him."

Sia put on the jacket. "Who couldn't you trust? Who
hurt you this badly that you kept seeking revenge?"

"The man who asked me to marry him, then left me
at the altar while he ran off with another woman. He
humiliated me."

She donned the pants and fastened them.

"Looks like you're out of clothes, but I'll give you
one for free, since I like a person who has spunk."

"Was your fiancé a pilot?"

"There's no flies on you, counselor…yet. Let's go."

"Where?"

Jackson responded by suddenly grabbing Sia's hair
and yanking her close. Her scalp was on fire; an instant
later she also felt the cold muzzle of the gun against her
temple. The voice next to her ear made her shudder.
"Do not test me more than you already have." Her fist
was still in Sia's hair, and tears sprang to the corners
of her eyes as Jackson gave it a vicious twist. "Now, I
will release you, and you will do as I say, when I say.
Are we on the same page?" To underscore the question,
she tugged harder on Sia's hair.

"Yes," she choked out.

"Good," she said quite pleasantly, and released her as suddenly as she'd grabbed her.

Sia staggered forward and landed hard on her hands and knees on the steel deck.

"Get up. Time is precious. We must go."

Sia obeyed for now. She opened her cabin door, but to her dismay there was no one in the gangway. "Which way do—" She had to break off, clear the sudden lump in her throat. "Which way?"

"Up to the deck."

"Outside? But the storm is in full force." She'd said it perhaps a bit too stridently, but her heart was pounding so hard she could hardly hear over it, and hysteria was edging up her throat, squeezing it tight.

"It's perfect for where we're going. I'm sure you'll remember it." She stepped closer and smiled, aiming the gun at her chest, and then lifting it to her head. "So let's stop wasting time, shall we?"

Sia swallowed hard, trying to remain calm. Panicking wouldn't save her.

She wasn't given time to comply before Maria grabbed her elbow and shoved her roughly ahead of her. "No more questions. No more answers. Not until we reach our destination. Then I'll grant you a few more."

Sia climbed the ladder to the upper deck. As she approached the hatch, she could hear the rain beating on the bulkhead, metallic echoes adding an eerie quality to an already surreal experience.

But she couldn't fool herself. She was in terrible danger. If she didn't do something, she was going to die. There was no doubt where Maria was taking her. Sia didn't know why, but she was sure of it.

"Open the hatch."

She gripped the wheel and applied pressure, the metal cold beneath her hands. It made barely a noise as it turned. Nothing but a whisper of a sound.

Pulling the door was another matter. "It's heavy," Sia said. "I need a hand."

"Don't get smart now, counselor."

"Do you want to be here all night while I struggle to get the door open?"

Maria sighed and jabbed the gun into Sia's back. Pain exploded, radiating down the back of her legs.

"That was just a reminder not to try anything."

As they pulled, the door swung inward and the sound of the rain and wind intensified until it was a pounding rhythm. Gusts of moisture coated Sia as she finally got the door open enough for them to see outside. Her breath caught in her throat at the violence of the sea, roiling with white-capped waves, the dark sky showing only flashes of lightning.

Thunder boomed and Sia jumped. Maria laughed at her discomfort.

"This is nothing compared to some storms I've seen," she said and she jabbed Sia with the muzzle of the gun again. Sia never wanted to hit someone as badly as she did now. "Pull the door closed and secure it."

Stepping out into the tempest drenched Sia straight through her heavy uniform coat. Icy rain poured down, pounding like nails on a roof, taking her breath away. The water was so heavy and came down so fast it almost made it difficult to breathe.

Sia knew she was not in sight of anyone on the bridge. It was a long shot, but if she could run far enough out onto the flight deck, maybe someone would see her from the bridge and send help.

She pulled at the door, her shoulder and arm muscles protesting as it swung slowly closed. She spun the wheel to lock the door in place. She tensed and like a runner off the mark she sprinted away from Maria. She was banking on the lack of visibility and the unsteady rolling of the deck to protect her from any gunshots. Sure enough none came, but Maria was obviously in just as good shape as Sia.

Fighting Maria was her only chance. She had no intention of dying without at least trying to save her own skin. It was about honor and principle. It was about survival.

Maria lunged at her, catching hold of her ponytail and jerking her back hard enough to make her teeth snap together. Sia shrieked in anger and pain and twisted toward Maria, lashing out with her feet, kicking at her knees, her shins, any part of her she could hit.

Maria's lips pulled back against her teeth in a feral snarl, and the back of her hand exploded against the side of Sia's face, snapping her head to the side, bringing a burst of stars behind her eyes and the taste of blood to her mouth. The sky and deck seemed to swirl, her arms flailing to futilely try to maintain her balance. She staggered sideways and fell. On her knees, she tried to scramble farther out onto the flight deck, well aware the lighted bridge was just above her. Adrenaline pumped through her like a drug, driving her forward even when Maria caught hold of her wrist and hauled her up and back, wrenching her sore shoulder.

But her struggles stilled automatically as the blade of a knife glinted off the flight deck lights.

Sia's heart drummed, impossibly hard, impossibly loud as the blade came nearer and nearer her face. It was a military knife, built for one thing and one thing only—killing. The blade was polished steel, the tip tapered and the edge serrated. Sia knew Maria had used this knife to kill once, and she had no doubt she would use it again.

"I would prefer if you would cooperate, Commander," she said, her face close to Sia's as she shouted over the sound of the rain. Maria's left hand slid along her jaw, fingers pressing into her flesh. The knife inched nearer.

The pitch of her voice was the same even tone that struck a nerve in Sia, but it was no longer devoid of emotion. Anger strummed through every carefully enunciated word as she brought the knife closer and closer. Sia's breath caught hard in her lungs as Maria touched the point of the knife to her cheek.

"Be a good, brave officer," she said, sliding the tip of the blade lightly downward. Over the corner of her mouth. "The Navy taught you how to do that, didn't they, Commander?"

Sia said nothing, afraid to speak, afraid to breathe as the blade traced down her chin, down the center of her throat to the vulnerable hollow at its base. If she struggled now, would Maria lose her patience and slice her throat and be done with her? That seemed preferable, but there were no guarantees. If she waited, bought time—even a minute or two—might she find another chance to break away?

She blinked the rainwater out of her eyes and wanted to groan. The bridge was directly above her. She could see movement, but no one glanced down, no one saw them.

The storm intensified, the rain falling harder, pelting the deck like bony fingers.

The knife rested in the V of her collarbone, the point tickling the delicate flesh above. The sensation made her want to gag. She swallowed back the need, felt the tip bite into her skin. The pain came seconds later, throbbing with her heartbeat. Blood slid down her neck to mix with the rain. Every cell of her body was quivering. Sia held back her fear and panic, grabbed her sanity with both mental hands and defied Maria with her eyes.

Maria laughed. "You have more courage than any man I've killed."

"Go to hell," Sia ground out between clenched teeth. She didn't even dare move her jaw with the knife so close to her throat.

"I've already been there. Now it's your turn." In one split second the knife was gone, but the gun was back in Maria's hand and she got quickly to her feet, hauling Sia with her. She pushed her hard in the back to get her to move forward. Sia almost lost her footing on the slick, heaving deck, but regained it at the last minute.

They skirted bridge and moved to the edge of the ship. When they reached a ladder that went down into the darkness, Maria said, "Go." But before Sia could comply, Maria grabbed her by the hair again, twisting brutally until Sia cried out. "If you try anything, I will shoot you in the back and throw your body overboard."

Sia looked up as Maria released her hair. She knew where Maria intended to take her.

The sponson.

Chris stalked away from Sia's cabin, his anger palpable. She was simply the most stubborn woman on the planet. She was hell-bent on saving her brother's memory and destroying any happiness she could have had.

She certainly wasn't doing it for Rafael. He was dead. Long dead. Sia was doing it to assuage her own sense of justice. She couldn't accept the fact that mistakes had been made and as a result he died.

The fact that she couldn't forgive him really had nothing to do with him at all. It was all about her own mission. The trouble was Chris needed it. He needed her to say the words. Needed it down to his battered soul, his broken heart.

He stopped and swung at the bulkhead, bruising his knuckles and sending pain down to his elbow in waves. But it felt good to have some outlet to release the tension roiling in him.

He was done with this. He had to be done with berating himself. He'd let Rafael go earlier, while he was on deck.

Why couldn't he let go of the need for Sia's forgiveness?

He didn't have to soul-search too long to realize why he needed Sia's forgiveness.

He knew why.

He was still in love with her, probably always would be. The pain of that admission made him want to run out on deck and howl at the storm.

He loved Sia just as much as he had six years ago. He'd never gotten over her.

Regardless of his anger and his sense of betrayal, he was in love with her. And he understood her better than he had six years ago when the feelings were raw and burned his gut like acid. It had never been about him. It had always been about her sense of loyalty to her family and to her brother.

Didn't mean her rejection didn't hurt. It did. Immensely. But the knowledge lessened it somewhat.

He headed to his stateroom and lay down on his bunk. Closing his eyes, the pitching and the rolling of the ship lulled him into sleep.

The buzzing of his phone roused him. Blearily he looked at the display, but didn't recognize the number. It had a Virginia area code.

He answered.

"Special Agent Vargas. This is Commander Soto's aide, Gabriel McBride, sir. I'm sorry to bother you, but I'm trying to track down the commander." The concern in the man's voice brought Chris up to a sitting position.

"She's in her stateroom. I left her less than a half hour ago."

"She's not responding to my calls or emails. I really need to speak to her. It's important."

His phone beeped impatiently to tell him he had an incoming call. When he saw it was Math, he said, "McBride. Hold on one second."

"Chris, check for your weapon."

"What?"

"Now, man. Check it now!"

At Math's urgent tone, Chris lurched out of bed to

tear open his locker. His sidearm was gone and his gut clenched hard.

"It's gone."

"The person who shot at you has it."

"How do you know that?"

"The bullets and the casings you sent me! The ballistics match your gun!"

"Son of a bitch. I've got to go."

Chris pinched the phone between his shoulder and ear as he frantically got dressed. He pressed the key to disconnect Math. "McBride. You have information regarding the case?" he asked urgently.

As soon as he was dressed, he bolted out the door, his lungs pumping with adrenaline and fear for Sia.

"Yes, I've got some information that ties the master chief to one of the crew members aboard. I think that's relevant to the case."

When he reached Sia's stateroom, he knocked, but there was no answer. His stomach sank when he tried the handle and discovered the door was open. The stateroom was empty.

"Agent Vargas, are you all right, sir?"

Chris realized McBride had spoken to him, but Chris had been distracted by the empty stateroom. Sia had to have been taken. There was nowhere for her to go. The ship was in lockdown.

"Yes, McBride, give me a minute."

His gaze snagged on Sia's computer. The laptop was open as if she'd been working on it, but the screen was dark. He went to it and pushed a button. The screen flashed on. He saw the website she'd visited. Then he noticed another file was open. He clicked it to open it.

When he saw the personnel list and the name the blinking cursor was on, he swore.

"Sir, what is it?"

"Tell me what tie you have to the master chief?"

"Well, when I was investigating him like the commander asked me to, I stumbled over some records…."

"McBride! The information!"

"The master chief was Lieutenant Maria Jackson's stepfather."

In a flash, memory came rushing back at him. She had been the LSO when he was aboard the *McCloud* and she'd been in the wardroom before he and Rafael had taken off. Both wingmen of the dead pilots remembered that she'd been in the wardroom before they had taken off. She was the one who had spiked their drinks, not Susan Cotes. The woman had been framed as she'd claimed. The scar, he remembered her scar. He remembered he'd gotten dizzy shortly after takeoff. His radar was messing up and he'd focused on it. Tried to see clearly, but his dizziness had gotten worse. Then he'd jerked at Rafael's voice in his ear and the plane had swerved, collided against his wingman's. Rafael had shouted an order, told him to eject as the jet spun out of control, whirling in midair. And it had been Chris's sense of survival that had saved him, that and his training as he lurched for the eject button and jettisoned from his impaired jet.

Jackson was the killer. She'd orchestrated the evidence against Susan Cotes. She framed her to distract and mislead them. She was the one who had taken his gun right before she'd come to them on the flight deck.

She must have shot at them when she'd left, then cleaned and replaced his gun in his locker. He was sure of it.

He was sure of one other thing. She was the one who had Sia and if he didn't find her, Jackson would kill her.

He closed his eyes and swore softly.

Sia shivered as her sodden dress uniform coat did nothing to keep her warm. Her back was pressed to the rail and the ocean churned below her, the waves breaking against the hull in white froth fury. There was no way to survive a plunge from this height. Even if she did, she wouldn't last a minute in the heaving waves below.

Suddenly the rain diminished and Sia faced fury of another kind.

"Do you know why I brought you up here?"

"No, but I'm guessing it has to do with the master chief."

"It does."

"Were you lovers?"

Maria tossed her head back and laughed. "God, no. He was too close to me for that. Or should I say too close to my mother."

"He was your father?"

"My stepfather."

"We were estranged for quite some time. Even when I was assigned to this ship, he didn't recognize me until I told him who I was. He was speechless and told me he wanted to make amends. As if he could. He left us, just like all men do. But—" her voice softened "—he did try to protect me. He took my GHB bottle and tried to kill you. He got scared when you said you were going to get the Navy to reopen your brother's case."

"So it wasn't his duty in the Navy that he tried to kill me. It was his duty to you as a father."

She shrugged. "It came to him later in life, when I was grown up, but I guess it counts for something."

"You're not going to get away with this."

"Yes, I will." With that she pulled aside a black tarp and Sia could see Lieutenant Cotes's dead eyes staring up at a night sky she would never see again. "It was supremely easy to spring her from jail. The master-at-arms was stupid enough to allow me a few moments with my friend. As soon as he turned his back, I grabbed his gun, forced him to unlock the door. I made him go inside and take off his pants. Then I shot him at point-blank range with his own gun. The look on his face was priceless. I wish I could have captured it on film."

"You made it look like he was going to…"

"That's right. No one would be surprised. Men are pigs." Maria pulled the tarp all the way off Susan's body. "She was a fighter, too. I had to be careful not to mark her."

Sia saw the blood on Susan's temple and the hole the bullet had left. "She didn't know she was rooming with a serial killer."

"It's not that black and white, but people like you need a classification. So you'll think what you want. She trusted me. Her mistake. She didn't know I was methodically framing her for Washington's murder. I even typed her suicide note on her computer and printed it out on her printer. It's beneath her body right now.

It is bad luck Chris had his accident when she wasn't on board. Then everything would have gone to plan."

"You're a monster!"

Maria laughed. "No, I'm not. I just need closure. You know all about that. That's what you've been searching for. That's what all the arguments were about with your boyfriend."

"I was searching for justice for my brother."

"Whatever your motives were, maybe now you can forgive your boyfriend. Oh, wait, no, that won't be possible. You'll be dead and he'll never know how you felt."

Her eyes hardened and Sia knew she was at the end of the line.

"Jump. There's no escape. At least it's more of a choice than you gave my stepfather."

Sia had only one chance and it was a very slim one. Her head jerked toward Susan's corpse. "Is she still breathing?"

Maria swung around to look at the body. Head down, Sia lunged for Maria, planting a shoulder hard in the woman's chest. The two of them landed on the hard steel, inches from Susan's dead face, and began wresting for control of the gun. Sia grabbed hold of Maria's arm and slammed it hard against the landing, but before she could shake the pistol loose, a white-hot pain sliced into her right side, momentarily shorting out all thought and strength.

Howling with pain and rage, she twisted around to find the source. The knife had penetrated the thick jacket and opened up a gash just below her rib cage.

Before Sia could react, Maria swung the gun up and slammed it into her temple.

* * *

Chris swore again and dropped his phone.

He knew where Sia had been taken at gunpoint—with his gun.

He raced out of the stateroom and swore under his breath as he wasted precious time opening the hatch and closing it behind him. He took a risk as he ran across the slippery, pitching deck only to lose his balance and slide to the edge, catching a spinning, stomach-dropping view of the ocean. He was able to stop his momentum by catching the rail. Breathing hard, rain sluicing down his face and soaked to the skin by the icy rain, he pulled himself up and made a beeline for the ladder. Reaching it, he descended frantically, his heart pounding with dread and fear for Sia. If he lost her... he couldn't complete the thought. Wouldn't accept she was already dead.

He reached the sponson and was just in time to see Maria push Sia's limp body over the edge.

Chapter 12

"Sia!" Chris screamed her name, and it snapped her out of the fog the blow to her head had caused. With her last ounce of strength, Sia snagged the rail with the crook of her elbow and struggled to hold on. The arm on her injured side was also weak from the shoulder injury, but she ignored the dull ache. Her feet dangled in empty air.

She panicked for a moment, and then realized she had to keep calm. She could hear Chris's roar of anger and the sound of battle above her. And she understood the cunning of the woman who had wanted him dead six years ago. It was ironic Jackson was now wrestling with the man who resembled the very fiancé who had walked away from her, just as Sia wrestled with her past. Her former fiancé was one smart, lucky guy, it seemed.

Her head cleared some more. Chris didn't know Maria had a knife.

Through sheer brute force and determination, Sia was able to get her body partially on the lip of the sponson. She could see a tangle of bodies as they struggled. Chris was intent on getting her to release the gun; he still didn't see the knife.

"Chris, she has a knife!" Sia screamed as loud as she could above the roar of the ocean and the storm.

He jerked away from her as she struck, the knife hitting empty air. Maria cursed as she looked at Sia and brought the gun up. Chris grabbed her gun hand and then also had to stop the momentum of her knife hand. He rose and pinned her, his knee on her chest.

Sia heard bones break and Maria cried out as she dropped the knife. It clattered to the deck and Chris dropped her hand to knock it away.

With an inhuman howl, Maria hit Chris in the face with a vicious blow. He was knocked to the side but his momentum stripped the gun out of her hand and it slid to the solid wall of the carrier with a ringing metallic sound.

Sia's arms were going numb and she was beginning to lose her grip. She couldn't hold on much longer. A huge, violent wave struck the ship and rolled over the flight deck, stinging her eyes. She lost her grip and slipped, crying out. Chris, distracted by the sound of her distress, looked her way, giving Maria the time she needed to go after the gun.

Chris yelled, "Hold on!" and scrambled after Maria a split second later. If he didn't end the fight soon, Sia was going to fall. Panic made her try to get better purchase on the rail, but the rain-slicked metal made it almost impossible.

Her head spun from the blow, her stomach lurched with nausea and her heart beat in time to her frantic breathing.

She looked up in time to see Chris catch Maria and deliver a powerful punch to her jaw. The woman flew back and landed heavily on Susan's body. Maria remained motionless, finally, thankfully, unconscious.

But it was too late for Sia. Her grip loosened and Chris was too far away. And her regrets piled up one on top of the other. She would never get the chance to tell him what was in her heart.

Her sight dimmed to gray and she started to fall away from the ship. Suddenly, without warning, her wrist was snagged with a warm hand and Chris's face was just above her. "Hang on, sweetheart, I got you."

Bracing his feet against the rail, he strained against her dead weight. With her head injury, she could barely help him at all. With a mighty heave of his powerful shoulders, he pulled her up and over the rail. She heard voices as men swarmed down the ladder and onto the sponson. Chris cradled her in his arms. She looked up at him wordlessly, her eyes shining with gratitude. But she couldn't maintain eye contact, couldn't utter a sound as her world turned to black.

Standing in sick bay, dripping water all over the immaculate deck, he watched as Sia was set on a gurney and wheeled away from him into a separate room. A crewman handed him a towel and gave a pointed look at it and the deck. Chris wiped his face and neck.

"Go get into some dry clothes," the captain said.

Chris didn't move.

"Go, Vargas. She'll be in there for a while. We have a very competent doctor."

Chris went back to his stateroom and showered off the rainwater and Sia's blood. He placed his clothes in evidence bags and zipped them shut. After dressing, he automatically reached for his firearm, but then remembered he'd had to turn it over to the Navy as evidence.

He went down to the brig and found Maria had regained consciousness. She didn't hold back and her sullen face only emphasized her cold and emotionless eyes as she confessed to everything. She'd be transferred from the ship and sent to Miramar, California, where she'd be then incarcerated at the Navy Consolidated Brig, or NAVCONBRIG.

His phone rang just as he was done and he headed back to sick bay. His boss asked him for an update, and Chris filled him in on all the details, leaving nothing out. He listened while his boss told him about a mission that required his expertise. He needed to leave the carrier right away. There would be a flight waiting for him in San Diego headed for Afghanistan.

He tried to protest, but his boss was firm. The *McCloud* case was wrapped up, he insisted. All that needed to be done was the paperwork.

Chris went back to his stateroom and packed. In one of the pockets of his suitcase, he pulled out his wings. He carried them wherever he went. Making his way back to sick bay, he found Sia in one of the bay's beds, still unconscious. She looked pale and so frail lying there. She had fought like a lion and he was so proud of her.

His throat was full as he stood there hoping for some

sign she would wake up. After several minutes, he could wait no longer. He didn't want to leave her like this, but he had no choice.

"Are you ready, Vargas?" the captain asked.

Sia came awake slowly. She could feel warm fingers stroking her face. Then at the material at her neckline, a rustling and then when the cloth was smoothed back a heaviness that hadn't been there before along with metal against her skin.

She struggled to come fully awake as she heard Chris's voice as he spoke in low tones to someone.

"No, I'll just be a few more minutes."

Sia wanted to open her eyes, wanted to make her mouth move, but she couldn't seem to throw off the lethargy. "That's for you, Sia. I've put the past behind me and no longer need them. Maybe my wings will let you soar and you will remember me from time to time."

He was leaving? No, she had something important to tell him. He couldn't go.

"How is she?"

That was the captain's voice.

"She's stable. I stitched up her side and she has a severe concussion. With rest, she should be fine." That unfamiliar voice must be the ship's doctor.

"And you, Vargas?"

"No worse for wear, sir. I appreciate the quick transportation. I have a case in Afghanistan that needs my attention. I just got the call from my superior. They have a transport waiting for me in San Diego."

"We'll be docking in about two hours, but the chopper is waiting for you."

She felt the stare of two men. "It's a good thing you arrived in time to save her. And her legalman should be commended for having the presence of mind to call the ship and alert me to the danger."

"Yes, sir. I've got to be going."

"Take care of yourself, Vargas."

"Thank you, sir."

Sia stirred and opened her eyes. No one was with her as she sat up, her side protesting. She was in a gown, lying in sick bay, an IV in her arm. Her head spun and she wondered how long it had been since Chris had left.

Without thinking, she pulled the IV out and swung her legs to the floor. Her knees buckled, but she pulled herself upright. Pain sliced into her side and her world spun, a terrible throbbing exploding in her head. She felt a heaviness at her neck and looked down. Chris had pinned his wings to her hospital gown and tears gathered in her eyes. She had to catch Chris. She had to talk to him. Now, in person.

She held on to the bulkhead as she made her way to the door and out into the gangway. She picked up speed as she headed for the flight deck. Sailors gaped at her as she passed in her hospital gown and bare feet, but she didn't care if her backside was hanging out.

She had to talk to Chris.

She reached the deck as her strength was waning. And saw him. She screamed his name, but all that she could get out was a croak. She ran a short distance to the deck, but Chris opened the helicopter door and set his bag inside. He followed it without looking back.

Sorrow filled her along with a healthy dose of shame and regret. "Chris," she said softly on a sob, clutching the wings in her hand, the edges biting into her palm. "Don't go." But as the doctor reached her, berating her for getting out of bed, Sia watched the chopper take off. She resisted as the doctor tried to get her back to sick bay. Watched until the chopper disappeared from her sight and Chris from her life.

She resisted the doctor's attempts to move her while time slipped away as she sat there questioning, remembering, hurting, mourning. She released all the tears she had held for Rafael, all the pain she had been so afraid to feel at his loss. It all came pouring out in a deluge, in a storm that shook her and drained her. She grieved alone. Just the way her brother had died. And on the deck of the carrier where he'd lived his last moments, she let go.

Chris faced forward, going on sheer determination. He was exhausted in the aftermath of apprehending Maria Jackson. She had confessed everything in a monotone voice, looking at him with accusing eyes as if she knew him.

In the end, just like her former fiancé, Chris had ruined everything.

He delivered the confession to the captain, who promised he would contact SECNAV and take care of expunging Chris's record of the pilot-error ruling.

Chris had told him not to bother, but he could see the captain wasn't going to heed his request. Chris agreed with the captain that it was important to clear Rafael's record.

It was the last thing he could do for Sia.

He turned his face away from the pilot as his eyes

filled. Blinking away the tears was much easier than trying to clear the pain from his heart. He knew where Sia stood and it was clear from their last conversation she could never forgive him. Regardless of who was responsible for Rafael's death, his jet had caused the accident. He felt raw at the thought that it was easier to forgive him when she thought he wasn't responsible for his actions that day. For him, it was too little, too late. He couldn't be with a woman who didn't fully believe in him and support him no matter what.

He loved her, but it was too late for them.

As the chopper zoomed through the now bright blue sky, Chris closed his eyes and let sleep take him. When he got to Afghanistan he would have to hit the ground running. Best to get the rest he needed now.

As he drifted into sleep, he couldn't help the memory of Sia's beautiful face from being the last thing he thought about before he succumbed to his fatigue.

Washington, D.C., in the spring was beautiful. A late spring had pushed the peak of the cherry blossoms to mid-May. Sia decided to walk from her hotel to Pennsylvania Avenue where the ceremony for her brother would be held. The sidewalk was packed with people celebrating Memorial Day.

Two months had passed since Sia had left the *U.S.S. James McCloud* and she was due back in San Diego in two months to testify at Lieutenant Maria Jackson's court-martial. There was really no need for a trial, since the woman had confessed. But testimony would be taken to strip the woman of her rank and insignia for the acts she'd committed against Navy personnel, along with the destruction of millions of dollars' worth of Navy property.

Sia felt that was wholly justified, as her side twinged from the knife cut that had almost fully healed.

She had made several inquiries into finding Chris, but NCIS was tight-lipped about where he was and had been uncooperative in granting her access to either his contact number or email. She had to wonder if that was because he had explicitly told them to keep his number private from her. She was shut out and would just have to wait until he returned from his mission.

The need to talk to him burned in her gut as she rounded a corner and saw the Navy Memorial across the street.

Stepping off the curb, she checked for traffic and crossed. She approached the rotunda that featured a granite sea map of the world, tall masts displaying signal flags, surrounded by fountain pools and waterfalls.

She approached the statue of The Lone Sailor and stood in front of it for a moment, remembering her brother, remembering his courage and his dedication to defending his country. She remembered his bright blue eyes and dark hair, his handsome, smiling face.

She remembered how she had striven to get him what he was due. A place where she could remember him for all times. A tangible place.

But the satisfaction of reaching her goal dimmed in the wake of what had happened between her and Chris aboard the *McCloud*.

She left the memorial and entered the exhibit area; another statue greeted her—a family embracing their loved one, home from the sea. Tears welled in Sia's eyes as she realized she would only be welcoming her brother home in spirit. For the first time, it was enough.

She located the room where the ceremony would take place and slipped in to take a seat in the second row. There was quite a crowd, all chattering as they settled in.

The ceremony started and a number of Navy personnel were honored. Then, when her brother's memorial was next on her program, she looked up to see the former and current captains of the *U.S.S. James McCloud* walk out onto the stage.

Her breath caught when Chris stepped out after them and seated himself. He looked impossibly handsome, even with beard stubble, his clothes wrinkled and his hair a tousled mess. His gray eyes were filled with pride and sadness.

The former captain of the *McCloud* got up and took the podium. "Today we are here to honor the fine men and women of the Navy. But there is one Naval officer who has been wronged by us. This we need to make amends for. Lieutenant Rafael Soto died when his fighter jet collided with Lieutenant Christophe Vargas's jet on a routine training mission over the Pacific. Unbeknownst to the Navy investigators at the time, the accident was really an attempted murder. Both pilots were sanctioned and had their records marred by a pilot-error ruling. Their records have now been cleared and we are here today to correct our error and honor Lieutenant Rafael Soto."

The captain finished his speech and left the podium. Chris rose, shook his hand and gave him a sharp salute. When he reached the podium, he looked out over the audience. "I am Christophe Vargas. I'm here today to tell you about my friend and wingman, Rafael Soto. He liked jelly beans and thought that Christmas was the best time of the year, more because of the giving than the receiving. He liked to garden and grow vegetables, saying a little dirt never hurt anyone. I don't have to tell any of you what it's like to lose someone who is as close to you as a brother. Some of you have lost a brother, sister, best friend. I carried around a lot of guilt for living when he died. For moving forward with my life. But after I was part of the investigative team to apprehend the person responsible for his death, it's been alleviated. I can't go back and change what happened. But I can honor the memory of my friend until the day I die. He was out there defending his country and I was proud to be at his side. Rafael," Chris said quietly, "I'll always have your six."

As Chris spoke, the lump in Sia's throat got tighter and tighter. Tears gathered in her eyes and she knew at that moment that she had been so wrong, even more than she had on the carrier when she'd tried to catch Chris. She had to talk to him.

He left the podium and sat down. The ceremony came to a close. In the crush of bodies, she was blocked from the stage. She frantically tried to find him, but lost him in the crowd.

Dejected and annoyed, she decided she would go to see Rafael's plaque. Chris would return to NCIS eventually and she'd go over to his office if she had to.

When she approached, she saw a man in rumpled clothing run his hand over the plaque, his head bowed. Her heart tripped and tears filled her eyes. Chris.

She took a few steps forward, suddenly tongue-tied. It took her a moment to find her voice. "Chris."

His head jerked up and he spun around. "Sia," he said, his eyes lighting up at the sight of her.

She smiled and came to him, afraid that if she touched him, he would disappear. They stood there for a few moments in awkward silence.

She looked up at him, her face carefully blank as she tried to assess the shift of feelings between them. "I've been looking for you."

"You found me."

"I wanted to thank you for saving my life. If you hadn't caught me—well, it seems to me that you were there when I needed you. Why is that, Chris? Even after I treated you so badly."

"You were grieving, Sia."

"I was, but what I forgot was that you were, too. At the time, when it was ruled an accident, I should have stood by you. I made a terrible mistake pushing you away, blaming you. I just needed my brother's life to have meant something, and you were part of what destroyed him. What I didn't realize at the time was that his life did have meaning."

Chris slipped an arm around her shoulders and eased her against him, pressing a kiss to the top of her head. It was all he needed to do and she marveled at his capacity to care. She splayed her hand against his warm chest, right over his heart, hoping against hope that she still held a place there.

"I know you didn't kill my brother and that you had no control over what happened."

"No, we know that Maria…"

She covered his mouth with her fingers. "No, Chris, it really doesn't have anything to do with her. This is between you and me. I have to ask you for your forgiveness for not believing in you, for not trusting you, for pushing you away when you needed me the most."

For a moment he looked stunned. He just stood there, waiting, staring past her. His chin trembled as he pressed his lips into a thin line. "My forgiveness?" he choked out.

"Yes. And if you can't, I'll wait," she promised. "I'll wait as long as you need me to wait. I want a future," she said simply, the wish so precious. "I want to go beyond the past. I want you to go with me."

"I forgive you."

"Just like that?" she said, her throat aching with unshed tears.

"Yes, because I already let go," he said, his voice deep and raw, his eyes trained on Rafael's plaque. "I refuse to let the past dictate how I will live my future. Not anymore. I forgave myself. So my forgiveness is easy. I never stopped loving you."

"What?"

"I love you, Sia."

Sia cupped his face and looked into his eyes. Seeing the truth there made her realize she had been wrong. There was more than hope that they could move on. She gave a shaky sigh of deep relief. "I love you, too. I never stopped, either. You are right. We need to put the past behind us. Move forward into the future. Our future."

Her arms went around his neck, her heart overflowing. She pressed her cheek against his chest and let go of everything, the past, the pain, the heartache and the terrible loss. She would always miss her brother and her family, but now, *now,* she finally let him go, let them go. Her gaze landed on his plaque and the tears were finally released. As they flowed, he lowered his mouth to hers for a kiss that was both bonding and beginning, promise and fulfillment…and love.

Hand in hand, they walked out of the building. When they hit the street, Chris smiled. "I sure hope you have a hotel room. I just got in from Afghanistan and didn't have time to check in."

It was Sia's turn to smile. She took his hand and this time she hailed a cab.

In her hotel room, she pushed the worn leather jacket off his shoulders, tugged his shirt loose and lifted it over his head. He raised his arms, accommodating her, and soon she had his bare chest at her disposal. To do with what she wanted.

And the hunger to do that was stirring in her blood.

She took it slowly. Sweetly, deliciously slowly.

He'd tasted her, taunted her, teased her, on several occasions. Now he would be at her command.

Her entire world narrowed down to the smooth expanse of honeyed skin wrapped oh-so-tautly across his chest. She dipped her head and drew her tongue slowly from his collarbone down the valley between his pecs, and then teased her way over to his nipple.

He drew in a sharp breath when she flicked her tongue across the sensitive tip. His hands came up to her hair, and she smiled as it came cascading down around her shoulders.

"If you like that move," he said, his mouth close to her ear, "you'll love what else I can do."

She laughed and looked deep into his eyes.

"Ambrosia," he said, "my Sia," his voice barely more than a rough whisper.

"Chris," she said, making his name a vow.

He cupped her head and slowly drew her mouth up to his, his eyes on hers as their lips met.

She took his kiss, letting her eyes drift shut as sensation after sensation poured through her. He slowly lowered them both to the bed, where he rolled her beneath him and continued his sweet seduction. Their clothes didn't come off in a frenzied rush, but with slow deliberation. As if they both needed to offset the harsh reality of what they'd been through with something pure and honest.

They took turns slowly exploring each other, delighting in discovering again what made them gasp, what made them moan. It was slow but complete capitulation where nothing was held back, nothing was hidden.

When she finally rolled to her back, taking his weight fully on top of her, it was as if she'd reached a golden point, a place she'd been trying to get to for a long, long time but could never quite find. That place where life suddenly became more complete and took on even greater meaning.

Without a word, they locked gazes and he slowly pushed into her, not stopping until she'd taken him fully inside of her. She wrapped her legs around him, holding him there, taking a moment to wallow, to revel a bit, in the supreme pleasure and contentment of being joined to that person who was to be hers.

And in that moment, despite all the fears, all the work yet to be done, and the promise of the future that lay before them, one thing was certain: her time spent with this man was going to mean something to her for the rest of her life.

The rest she let go, and willed herself just to feel, to truly live purely in that moment and that moment only. She moved first, pressing her hips up into his. He began to move inside of her, so deep, filling her so perfectly. It wasn't wild, it wasn't frenzied; it was powerful and necessary. He slid one arm beneath the small of her back and lifted her hips even higher so he could sink into her even more deeply. Their gazes caught, held, and their thrusts came faster, deeper. She watched him climb, watched as his need for her strengthened, felt his muscles gather and bunch as he drew ever closer. She tightened around him, needing to know she could take him to that place, give him that sweet bliss that he so effortlessly gave her, and found herself shuddering, too, in intense satisfaction as he growled through a pulsing release.

He kissed her, pressed another kiss to her temple, and then dropped another one just below her ear before rolling to his back, pulling her with him, and settling her body alongside his.

She fell against him with her body as she'd fallen for him with her heart. She didn't question it. Her eyes were already drifting shut as she shifted enough to press a soft kiss over his heart before tucking her arm across his body. Then she draped her leg across his, needing him as close to her as he could get.

It was okay to let go completely; he was there to catch her.

"Chris," she said as the light faded from outside and the city quieted.

"Yes," he murmured.

"In case I forgot to say it. I for—"

He covered her mouth with a kiss, his lips soft and warm. "I know."

Epilogue

"Chris," she puffed, "wait for me." He turned and smiled at her.

"Well, come on, slowpoke." He waited while she slipped her arm through his.

She huffed in mock anger. "You're not carrying around a bowling ball in your stomach, mister, so just be patient with your pregnant wife," she said, laughing as she made the last few steps to the rotunda of the Navy Memorial.

"I said to wait until after the baby was born to do this. You, on the other hand, acted quite unreasonable. 'No, Chris,'" he mimicked in a high falsetto voice, "'I have to be there on the anniversary of my brother's memorial.'"

She laughed until she was breathless. "You know this is important to me, so you even drove me all the way from Norfolk. It was just a few hours' drive, anyway, and I'm not due for another two weeks."

He looked down at her enormous stomach and sent his hand lovingly over the huge mound. "It feels risky to me."

He held her hand as they made their way to the plaque. She stood in front of it and smiled at the handsome picture of her brother. Gently, she ran her hands over the words: *In honored memory of Lieutenant Rafael Soto, loving brother and son, keeper of freedom and liberty, and lover of jelly beans.*

He would have been happy for his sister and his best friend. Sia and Chris had been married now for two years. Two wonderful years. It hadn't been smooth sailing that whole time, mostly because she was stubborn, but Chris had always been there for her and she for him.

Suddenly the dull ache she'd had in her back all the way from Norfolk intensified. There was a popping sound and a rush of water that left a puddle beneath her.

Several people were milling around the other memorials and they turned to look at her. One woman covered her mouth as her husband whipped out his cell phone and dialed.

"Oh, damn," Chris said, looking down, then looking at her. "Is that what I think it is?"

She smiled, not at all panicked as she took Chris's hand. "Yes. We're going to have a baby." Chris didn't move, just stared at her, dumbfounded. "Now, Chris."

"Right, hospital."

He took her hand and started to pull her when a strong contraction took hold of her, sending pain across her abdomen and stabbing into her lower back. She doubled over and several people asked Chris if he needed help. He just shook his head and waited out her contraction.

When it was over, Sia knew. "Ah, Chris, we're not going to make it to the hospital."

"Oh, damn," he said again as he looked frantically for a place to set her down. "That bench." He dragged her over and helped her lie down. He settled her jacket over her hips and legs as he removed clothing to make way for the baby.

"I think I've been in labor all day," she said, breaking off as another searing contraction tightened her stomach into a hard knot of pain. She cried out and Chris went white.

"Hang on, honey."

"I didn't know it was labor pains," she panted. "They were so mild."

"You're just one of the lucky ones."

She cried out as another strong band of pain contracted and she felt a pressure in her groin. "I feel the need to push," she said, the unmistakable feeling of bearing down overwhelming her.

"Then push, honey. I'm here."

Sia let her body take over, since it seemed to know what it wanted to do.

After several minutes, Chris cried out, "I can see the head. Keep going." He ripped off his jacket and his T-shirt.

Sia continued to push and Chris asked her to stop momentarily as he navigated the shoulders. She could hear the sound of an ambulance in the distance. She remembered someone had called for one when they saw her water break. But they were going to be too late as she felt her child slide from her body. Chris caught the small bundle in his hands and wrapped the baby in the soft cotton of his shirt as Sia heard the first cries.

"It's a boy," Chris said, looking up at her with a joyous expression on his face, wonderment in his eyes. And Sia reached down and touched her son. The little boy turned his head, and, like lightning, Sia was struck with instantaneous love, a bond that filled her with the same wonder she'd just seen on her husband's face.

She stroked his head and said softly as the paramedics rushed up to them, "Hello, Rafael."

* * * * *

COMING NEXT MONTH from Harlequin®
Romantic Suspense
AVAILABLE JULY 24, 2012

#1715 CAVANAUGH RULES
Cavanaugh Justice
Marie Ferrarella
Two emotionally closed-off homicide detectives take a chance on love while working a case together.

#1716 BREATHLESS ENCOUNTER
Code X
Cindy Dees
A genetically enhanced hero on a mission to draw out modern-day pirates rescues the woman who may actually be their target.

#1717 THE REUNION MISSION
Black Ops Rescues
Beth Cornelison
A black ops soldier and the woman who once betrayed him confront their undeniable attraction while he guards her and a vulnerable child in a bayou hideaway.

#1718 SEDUCING THE COLONEL'S DAUGHTER
All McQueen's Men
Jennifer Morey
It's this operative's mission to bring a kidnapped woman home. Will the headstrong daughter of a powerful colonel take his heart when he does?

You can find more information on upcoming Harlequin® titles, free excerpts and more at www.Harlequin.com.

HRSCNM0712

REQUEST YOUR FREE BOOKS!
2 FREE NOVELS PLUS 2 FREE GIFTS!

◆ Harlequin®

ROMANTIC
SUSPENSE

Sparked by Danger, Fueled by Passion.

YES! Please send me 2 FREE Harlequin® Romantic Suspense novels and my 2 FREE gifts (gifts are worth about $10). After receiving them, if I don't wish to receive any more books, I can return the shipping statement marked "cancel." If I don't cancel, I will receive 4 brand-new novels every month and be billed just $4.49 per book in the U.S. or $5.24 per book in Canada. That's a saving of at least 14% off the cover price! It's quite a bargain! Shipping and handling is just 50¢ per book in the U.S. and 75¢ per book in Canada.* I understand that accepting the 2 free books and gifts places me under no obligation to buy anything. I can always return a shipment and cancel at any time. Even if I never buy another book, the two free books and gifts are mine to keep forever.

240/340 HDN FEFR

Name _____ (PLEASE PRINT) _____

Address _____ Apt. # _____

City _____ State/Prov._____ Zip/Postal Code _____

Signature (if under 18, a parent or guardian must sign) _____

Mail to the **Reader Service:**
IN U.S.A.: P.O. Box 1867, Buffalo, NY 14240-1867
IN CANADA: P.O. Box 609, Fort Erie, Ontario L2A 5X3

Not valid for current subscribers to Harlequin Romantic Suspense books.

Want to try two free books from another line?
Call 1-800-873-8635 or visit www.ReaderService.com.

* Terms and prices subject to change without notice. Prices do not include applicable taxes. Sales tax applicable in N.Y. Canadian residents will be charged applicable taxes. Offer not valid in Quebec. This offer is limited to one order per household. All orders subject to credit approval. Credit or debit balances in a customer's account(s) may be offset by any other outstanding balance owed by or to the customer. Please allow 4 to 6 weeks for delivery. Offer available while quantities last.

Your Privacy—The Reader Service is committed to protecting your privacy. Our Privacy Policy is available online at www.ReaderService.com or upon request from the Reader Service.

We make a portion of our mailing list available to reputable third parties that offer products we believe may interest you. If you prefer that we not exchange your name with third parties, or if you wish to clarify or modify your communication preferences, please visit us at www.ReaderService.com/consumerschoice or write to us at Reader Service Preference Service, P.O. Box 9062, Buffalo, NY 14269. Include your complete name and address.

HRS11B

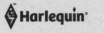

Werewolf and elite U.S. Navy SEAL, Matt Parker, must set aside his prejudices and partner with beautiful Fae Sienna McClare to find a magic orb that threatens to expose the secret nature of his entire team.

Harlequin® Nocturne presents the debut of beloved author Bonnie Vanak's new miniseries, PHOENIX FORCE.

Enjoy a sneak preview of THE COVERT WOLF, available August 2012 from Harlequin® Nocturne.

Sienna McClare was Fae, accustomed to open air and fields. Not this boxy subway car.

As the oily smell of fear clogged her nostrils, she inhaled deeply, tried thinking of tall pines waving in the wind, the chatter of birds and a deer cropping grass. A wolf watching a deer, waiting. Prey. Images of fangs flashing, tearing, wet sounds…

No!

She fought the panic freezing her blood. And was gradually able to push the fear down into a dark spot deep inside her. The stench of Draicon werewolf clung to her like cheap perfume.

Sienna hated glamouring herself as a Draicon werewolf, but it was necessary if she was going to find the Orb of Light. Someone had stolen the Orb from her colony, the Los Lobos Fae. A Draicon who'd previously been seen in the area was suspected. Sienna had eagerly seized the chance to help when asked because finding it meant she would no longer be an outcast. The Fae had cast her out when she turned twenty-one because she was the bastard child of a sweet-faced Fae and a Draicon killer. But if she found the Orb, Sienna could return to the only home she'd known. It also meant she could recover her lost memories.

Every time she tried searching for her past, she met with a closed door. Who was she? Which side ruled her?

Fae or Draicon?

Draicon, no way in hell.

Sensing someone staring, she glanced up, saw a man across the aisle. He was heavily muscled and radiated power and confidence. Yet he also had the face of a gentle warrior. Sienna's breath caught. She felt a stir of sexual chemistry.

He was as lonely and grief stricken as she was. Her heart twisted. Who had hurt this man? She wanted to go to him, comfort him and ease his sorrow. Sienna smiled.

An odd connection flared between them. Sienna locked her gaze to his, desperately needing someone who understood.

Then her nostrils flared as she caught his scent. Hatred boiled to the surface. Not a man. Draicon.

The enemy.

Find out what happens next in THE COVERT WOLF by Bonnie Vanak.

Available August 2012 from Harlequin® Nocturne wherever books are sold.

Harlequin® Super Romance®

*Enjoy a month of compelling, emotional stories, including
a poignant new tale of love lost and found from*

Sarah Mayberry

When Angela Bartlett loses her best friend to a rare heart
condition, it seems only natural that she step in and help
widower and friend Michael Young. The last thing she
expects is to find herself falling for him....

Within Reach

HARLEQUIN
RECOMMENDED
Read!

Available August 7!

Find more great stories this month from
Harlequin® Superromance® at

www.Harlequin.com

HSRSM71795